FITZWIZO
and the
GOOD GHOST GUIDE

FITZWIZO

and the
GOOD GHOST GUIDE

LINDA PITT

Andersen Press · London

First published in 1999 by
Andersen Press Limited,
20 Vauxhall Bridge Road, London SW1V 2SA

British Library Cataloguing in Publication Data available
ISBN 0 86264 865 3

Cover illustration and vignette © 1999 by Bridget MacKeith

Typeset by FSH, London WC1
Printed and bound in Great Britain by the Guernsey Press Company Ltd.,
Guernsey, Channel Islands

For Dennis

One

Fitzwizo, full title Sir Frederick Fitzwizo, was feeling restless. Sometimes, it's not much fun being a ghost – especially if most of your haunting is done at a place like Coldhill Castle.

This castle, as you might guess, stood on a hill – a high, cold hill. At this time of year the wind whipped around what was left of the ancient towers and walls. Fitzwizo could stand it no longer.

'Marigold!' he called to his wife. 'I'm just popping into town. Won't be long.'

Lady Marigold Fitzwizo, she of the long golden tresses, came floating dreamily through the wall. She was a good floater. The thickest of castle walls presented no problem to her.

'Very well, Frederick dear,' she said. 'Why don't you take Fen along with you? She's in one of her moods.'

Fitzwizo sighed. He loved his daughter Fenella very dearly but, like all teenagers, she could be a bit of a pain at times.

'What's the matter with her now?'

'Oh, you know – the usual sort of thing. Flouncing about. Complaining about being bored. Arguing with Percy.'

Fitzwizo sighed again. *No one* should be condemned to have teenage children for all these years – hundreds of years so far. It was too much for any parent to bear!

'Oh, all right,' he agreed, 'I'll take her with me.'

You may, at this point, be wondering how it was that Fitzwizo and his daughter were able to leave Coldhill Castle at all. Most ghosts, as you know, are tied to one place.

The Fitzwizos, in their lifetime and after, were a most unusual family. It was said (although Lady Marigold tried to keep this quiet) that some distant ancestors had been wizards – hence the family name. It was certainly true that at least one Fitzwizo in each generation did possess unusual powers.

So it was that Fenella and her father were not confined to Coldhill Castle. They could get out and about and do their haunting in different places. Lady Marigold and Percival could not. Mind you, Lady Marigold and her son never seemed to *want* to leave their ancestral home – which was just as well.

'Fenella!' called Lady Marigold. 'Your father would like you to go into town with him.'

Fenella Fitzwizo came flouncing over from the East Tower, followed by her brother Percival. With her flaming red hair and burning cheeks, she did not look at all ghostly. She was very angry.

'I'm fed up with Percy!' she fumed. 'He's a pompous twit!'

'Language, dear,' murmured Lady Marigold. 'I really don't know where you pick up these expressions.'

'It all comes from going into town with Father, of course,' said Percival. 'I wouldn't be seen dead in that place, among all those common people.'

'No,' sneered Fenella, 'you'd rather be seen dead here, wouldn't you? You're so boring – just like this boring, gloomy old castle.'

'You are talking about Coldhill Castle,' said Percival, drawing himself up to his full height (which wasn't very high). 'Do not forget that this is the ancestral home of the Fitzwizos.'

Fen's right, thought her father. Percy really is a pompous twit. He did not, of course, say so. After all, Percival was his only son – apple of his mother's eye.

Lady Marigold's delicate white hand fluttered up to her forehead. 'Do something, Frederick! I can't stand any more of this! I can feel one of my headaches coming on.'

Fitzwizo cleared his throat. 'Now, look here, you two!' he said in his sternest voice. (He was not very good at being stern.) 'You must stop this at once. You're giving your mother a headache.'

'It was all Fen's fault,' said Percival. 'She started it.'

'No, I didn't! I just got mad because...'

'Are you coming to town or not, Fen?' her father interrupted hastily. 'Because I'm going – NOW!'

'Of course I'm coming. I can't wait to get out of this mouldy old place.'

'Good!' said Percival. 'Mother and I will have some peace and quiet at last.'

'You're welcome to it,' snapped Fenella. 'I'm sick of peace and quiet. Let's go, Dad!'

Down in the valley was the new town of Coldhill, named after the castle. It was a very new town, with no old buildings in sight – not counting the ancient castle on the hill.

Fitzwizo loved it. He and Fenella spent many happy hours drifting in and out of houses, shops and offices. They were (as I may remind you from time to time) unseen and unheard. Not one person in that busy town knew anything about these visitors from another age.

Fitzwizo was fed up with the Middle Ages. He had had enough of old, cold, draughty places. Here, in Coldhill, there were buses, cars, computers, television – all the comforts and delights of the twentieth century.

For, although they had been around for such a long time, Fitzwizo and his daughter were very modern ghosts – well, modern in spirit anyway!

Two

In a brand new office block in the town of Coldhill there was a brand new government department. The new head of that department, Ms Jane Grimwood, was about to arrive.

Professor Archibald Pond and his assistant, Amanda Day, were not looking forward to her arrival. They had heard all about Ms Grimwood.

'She's been sent here,' said Mandy glumly, 'because they couldn't stand her at her last office. She drove them all mad.'

'That's just gossip, Mandy,' said Professor Pond. 'We haven't even met this woman yet. She might turn out to be very nice.'

'Now's your chance to find out,' whispered Mandy. 'Here she comes!'

A tall, dark-haired woman strode into the room. She slammed her briefcase down on the desk and stared at them scornfully.

'I am Ms Jane Grimwood, your new head of department. I understand that you two are to be my entire
team.'

'Yes, I am Professor Archibald Pond and this is my
assistant, Amanda Day.'

Mandy said nothing. She knew already that she was
not going to like their new boss. Everything that she had
heard was true.

'Not much of a department!' sniffed Ms Grimwood.
'One retired university professor and one young school
leaver. I had hoped for better.'

'I think you'll find,' Professor Pond said gently, 'that
Mandy and I are hard-working and efficient.'

'I should hope so!' snapped Ms Grimwood. She sat
down, opened her briefcase and took out some papers. 'I
intend to put this department on the map. We must get
down to work at once.'

At that moment Fitzwizo and Fenella drifted into the
room. I'm sure I don't have to remind *you* that they were
unseen and unheard. But, believe me, some readers do
forget this sort of thing – and it is rather important!

As they entered the room (and this often happens with
ghosts) the temperature dropped by a few degrees.

'Strange!' said Ms Grimwood, shivering. 'It's
suddenly got colder.'

'It does that from time to time,' said Mandy, turning
up the radiator. 'It happens in the other offices as well.
Even the heating experts can't explain it.'

'If they can't explain it,' declared Ms Grimwood,

'they are not experts. There is an explanation for everything. However, we must get down to business.'

'They're just having a boring old meeting,' complained Fitzwizo. 'They're not even using the computers. Come on, Fen! Let's...'

'Wait, Dad! Listen!'

'As you know,' Ms Grimwood was saying, 'Ofspook is a new division of the Department of Tourism. It seems, for some strange reason, that tourists are becoming more and more interested in ghosts. Our mission is to investigate and report on ghostly activity in our area. This branch of Ofspook will visit various sites in Middleshire. The results will be published in the *Good Ghost Guide*.'

'Will they get stars?' asked Mandy. 'Like hotel guides?'

'Apparently,' said Ms Grimwood scornfully, 'the symbol is to be a tiny phantom. Not my idea, as you can imagine.'

'I like the idea of a tiny phantom,' laughed Mandy. 'It's different. I think it's cute.'

'Cute!' sneered Ms Grimwood. 'Well, I expect that many tourists are just like you, Ms Day. No doubt that's why they picked such a childish symbol. But now we must get down to the business in hand – how to award them.'

She handed each of them a printed sheet. 'Please pay attention, both of you, while we go over the Ofspook guidelines.'

Slowly she read:

Symbols are to be awarded in the following categories:

A. GHOSTLY SOUNDS
One or two phantoms may be awarded for any strange, unexplained sounds, e.g. footsteps, screams, moans.

B. GHOSTLY SIGHTINGS
One or two phantoms may be awarded for any unusual sightings, e.g. people or scenes from the past.

C. GHOSTLY ATMOSPHERE
One phantom may be awarded for general atmosphere – a strong sense of the past.

Here she paused and gave them a sharp look. 'Have you any questions about these guidelines?'

'What if there are a lot of sightings in one place?' asked the professor. 'Does it still get no more than two phantoms in that category?'

'Such a thing is most unlikely to happen, Professor Pond. However, we at Ofspook have thought of it. In that case, we may award starred phantoms – the symbol would have a small star above it.'

'So it's possible for somewhere to get five starred phantoms?' asked Mandy.

'Quite *impossible*, I would say,' sniffed Ms Grimwood.

'But we shall see. We start our investigations tomorrow. I have arranged for both of you to visit Dingley Hall in the afternoon and to stay there overnight.'

'Do *you* believe in ghosts, Ms Grimwood?' asked Mandy.

'That,' snapped Ms Grimwood, 'is none of your business, Ms Day. As far as I am concerned, ghosts may or may not exist. I do not know and I do not care. What matters is that I have been asked to manage this department and I shall do so with my usual efficiency.'

'Are we going to visit Coldhill Castle?' asked Professor Pond.

At the mention of his own home, Fitzwizo felt the hairs at the back of his neck stand on end.

'Aren't they planning to knock that down and build a large hotel on the site?' asked Ms Grimwood, consulting her list. 'I don't suppose Ofspook will bother with...oh, yes, here it is. I shouldn't think you'll find much of interest in that boring old ruin.'

'Boring old ruin yourself!' hissed Fenella. (Just as well that she couldn't be heard!) 'Anyway, they haven't decided about that hotel yet, have they, Dad?'

'No, but they were discussing it again at the last council meeting.' (Fitzwizo tried to attend all the meetings of the town council. He liked to know what was going on in Coldhill.)

'Coldhill Castle is by no means a complete ruin,' said Professor Pond. 'Much of the East Tower is still standing and some of the West Tower. Many of the

9

remaining walls are in quite good condition.'

'Surely they couldn't demolish it!' protested Mandy. It's *our* castle! It's important!'

'I know,' sighed the professor. 'The trouble is, it attracts so few visitors these days.'

'Well, they can't knock it down if it gets into the *Good Ghost Guide*,' declared Mandy. 'Lots of visitors will come if it gets some phantoms – especially some starred phantoms.'

'By Jove!' cried Fitzwizo excitedly, clutching Fenella's arm. 'She's right, Fen! We'll get our phantoms. We'll save Coldhill Castle! Come on, let's go! We must tell your mother and Percy about this – at once!'

As always, when he was whirling through the air towards Coldhill Castle, Fitzwizo wished that his distant ancestors had invented a more comfortable form of travel. This felt like being in the middle of a mini whirlwind – all very well for those old wizards perhaps, but not for him. It always left him feeling slightly dizzy.

In town, of course, he could use modern transport. He loved travelling in buses and cars. To get up and down the hill, however, he and Fenella had to make use of the old whirling technique. Nowadays, no buses and very few cars made their way up the hill to Coldhill Castle.

'Mum! Percy!' shouted Fenella as they slowed down and landed. 'Come quick! We've got some really important news.'

Her mother came floating anxiously through the wall. 'They're going to demolish us, aren't they, Frederick? They're going to build that dreadful modern hotel?'

Lady Marigold was a great worrier. At the moment this was her greatest worry. Fitzwizo knew that he should never have told her about it. Still, now he could put her mind at rest.

'You don't have to worry any more,' he declared. 'We, the Fitzwizos, are going to save Coldhill Castle. Trust me, Marigold. That hotel will never...'

'I hope this is *really* important,' Percival complained loudly as he joined them. 'I was just putting on my armour.'

Percival was very proud of his first full suit of armour. He spent most of his time polishing it, putting it on and clanking about in it. Today, he had just got as far as the breastplate and was carrying his helmet under his arm.

'This is very important,' said Fenella. 'Dad will tell you all about it.'

'And so,' said Fitzwizo, when he had explained everything, 'we have got to get as many starred phantoms as we can. Then we'll have lots of visitors and Coldhill Castle will be saved.'

'It would be nice to have more visitors,' Lady Marigold said wistfully. 'We used to get quite a lot.'

'That was before they built the Adventure Park,' said Fenella. 'They all want to go there now.'

'Can't blame them, I suppose,' said Fitzwizo,

11

forgetting himself. 'That park is great fun, you know. I love the log flume and the ghost train and...'

'Ghost train!' shrieked Lady Marigold. 'You never told me about going on any ghost train, Frederick. How *could* you?'

'It was just a bit of fun, dear. Very silly, of course – not at all like the real thing.' He chuckled. 'Once I materialised in full armour, right beside this silly woman who kept saying she didn't believe in ghosts. That gave her a bit of a...'

'FATHER!' Percival was at his most disapproving. 'We were talking about Coldhill Castle – not some common amusement park. How could you possibly compare them?'

'I wasn't *comparing* them,' Fitzwizo protested. 'I was just saying...'

'Boring old ruin, indeed!' growled Percival. 'How *dare* that woman insult the ancestral home of the Fitzwizos!'

'I agree,' said Fenella.

Her brother stared at her in amazement. 'You agree? With me? Who called it *boring* and *gloomy* only this morning?'

'Yes...well...that was this morning. Anyway, it's all right for *me* to say it, but not that horrible Ms Grimwood.'

'Now, look here, you two,' said Fitzwizo in his sternest voice. 'Stop arguing! We must make plans, work out our strategy.'

'Sorry, Dad,' said Fenella. 'We're listening.'

Fitzwizo cleared his throat importantly. 'After much thought, I have decided to call our plan *Operation Phantom*. They always call them that sort of thing on television.' (Fitzwizo was mad about police programmes!) 'What do you think?'

'I like it,' said Fenella enthusiastically. 'Reminds me of that programme we watched last week – remember, Dad?' She put on a deep voice, 'And now, viewers – will *Operation Phantom* succeed? Does it have the ghost of a chance? To find out, tune in to…'

'I was thinking,' Fitzwizo interrupted hastily, 'of the more serious police programmes, Fenella – such as…'

Percival groaned loudly. '*Nothing* will succeed if you two keep going on about your stupid television programmes. At this rate we won't even get *half* a phantom.'

'Not even half a phantom!' moaned Lady Marigold. 'I couldn't bear it, Frederick. The disgrace!'

'Don't you worry, Mum,' said Fenella, glaring at her brother. 'We'll get our phantoms. We'll get more phantoms than anyone else in the *Good Ghost Guide*. Won't we, Dad?'

'Of course we will,' agreed Fitzwizo. 'We'll work out a strategy. We'll meet our targets. When that Ofspook team comes to Coldhill Castle, we'll be ready for them!'

Three

Next morning Fitzwizo was up bright and early, all ready for *Operation Phantom*. 'It's like setting off for a battle or a tournament,' he announced gleefully as he struggled with his armour. 'I haven't felt like this for hundreds of years.'

'You're *not* wearing full armour, Dad!' Fenella was horrified. 'I can't *bear* all that clanking about! It's embarrassing!'

'But I can't just wear my ordinary clothes, Fen!' protested her father. 'This is a sort of battle, after all. I have to be prepared. The honour of the Fitzwizos is at stake.'

'What about that nice coat of chain mail, dear?' suggested Lady Marigold. 'You know – the one your father gave you. You haven't worn that for centuries. It's much lighter and it *does* suit you, Frederick.'

Fitzwizo brightened. 'You're right, my dear, as usual. What do you think, Fen?'

Fenella sighed. 'Oh, all right, Dad. If you must!'

14

'Now do be careful, both of you,' said Lady Marigold anxiously. 'And remember, Frederick, you're not as young as you used to be.'

When Fitzwizo and Fenella arrived at the office, Ms Grimwood was sitting at her desk, issuing instructions to Professor Pond and Mandy. 'As you both know, Dingley Hall is a very splendid Elizabethan house. This afternoon you will mingle with the other visitors – get the feel of the place.'

'Get into the *spirit* of the thing, you mean,' giggled Mandy.

Ms Grimwood ignored Mandy's little joke. 'For your overnight stay you have permission to use the kitchen as your base. As you know, when you have an overnight investigation, you do not come in to work on the following day. You will report back to me on Friday morning.'

'And what will you be doing?' asked Professor Pond before he could stop himself.

'*DOING?*' Ms Grimwood sprang to her feet. If looks could kill, the professor would have been dead on the spot. 'How *dare* you ask what I shall be doing? I am a *manager.* I don't *do.* I manage. I organise. I am in charge. It's a very important job.'

'I'm sorry.' Professor Pond was a gentle man. He did not like anger. 'I didn't mean…'

'Very well.' Ms Grimwood sat down stiffly. 'We will discuss your findings, if any, on Friday morning.'

*

As they drove to Dingley Hall, Professor Pond and Mandy were not aware of their two extra passengers. Fitzwizo and Fenella had settled comfortably into the back seat of the professor's car – Fitzwizo's favourite form of transport.

'I'd better turn up the heating,' said the professor. 'It's colder that I thought.'

'Just like the office,' said Mandy. 'It's not at all cold outside.'

'Perhaps they're both haunted,' joked the professor. 'You never know!'

'A haunted office block!' laughed Mandy. 'A haunted car! Who would believe us?'

'I would,' chuckled Fenella, nudging her father. 'What do you say, Dad?'

Fitzwizo wasn't saying anything. He was fast asleep. He stayed fast asleep throughout the journey to Dingley Hall – exhausted after a restless night and his early morning whirl down the hill.

'Wake up, Dad!' Fenella dug him in the ribs. 'We're here!'

'*Here*?' Fitzwizo woke up with a start. He stared wildly around. 'Where? My horse? My lance? Where am I?'

'Oh, Dad!' sighed Fenella. 'We're at Dingley Hall. *Operation Phantom*. Remember?'

'Oh, yes. Sorry, Fen. I was just dreaming about the old days – the old battles.'

16

'Never mind the old days, Dad. We've got our own battles to fight – right now! Come on! We must catch up with Mandy and the professor.'

Professor Pond and Mandy had joined a party of school children who were clustered around the entrance to the house.

'Keep together, 5J,' their teacher was saying, 'and listen carefully to our guide. You won't forget what I said about good behaviour, will you?'

'No, Mr Jones,' chorused 5J.

A lady, wearing a guide's badge, came bustling out of the house. She smiled brightly at them. 'Good afternoon. I am your guide, Mrs Kane. And you must be Mr Jones, with 5J from Brookside Primary School?'

Mr Jones confirmed this and Mrs Kane turned to Mandy and the professor. 'I take it that you are Professor Pond and Ms Day? I have been told that you are to join our tour this afternoon. I hope you will find it of interest.'

'I'm sure we will,' said Professor Pond. 'We look forward to it.'

'And now, children,' gushed Mrs Kane, 'I'm sure that you are all very excited about your visit to Dingley Hall – aren't you?'

'Yes, Mrs Kane,' chanted 5J.

'This house,' explained their guide as she led them into the spacious entrance hall, 'was built during the reign of Queen Elizabeth the First. It is one of the finest examples of an Elizabethan house in the whole country.'

Fenella looked around with interest. She stared at the beautiful tapestries, the heavy carved furniture, the portraits on the walls. She knew, of course, that Coldhill Castle was very very old. She knew that the town of Coldhill was very very new. But Fenella remembered little about all those centuries in between. She listened carefully to what their guide was telling them.

'And now we come to the main stairs,' said Mrs Kane, as they approached the wide, shallow, stone steps. 'This famous staircase is said to be haunted by the ghost of Alice, Countess of Middleshire.' Mrs Kane gave a light laugh. 'Of course *we* don't really believe in ghosts, do we, children?'

'I do,' a sharp-eyed little girl piped up. 'I've seen them – often.'

'Oh, no!' groaned Fitzwizo. 'Not one of those!'

For he knew that there were some people, often children, who *could* see ghosts – even when the ghosts did not choose to materialise. Such people were a great nuisance. Fortunately, they were not often believed.

'Now, Belinda,' said Mr Jones, 'you know that's not true.'

'It is,' insisted Belinda, pointing in the direction of Professor Pond and Mandy. 'I can see two of them over there – a man and a girl.'

'Belinda!' scolded Mr Jones. 'Remember what I said about manners! You must apologise to…'

'Excuse me,' interrupted Professor Pond. 'Would you

mind if I asked Belinda a few questions, Mr Jones?'

Mr Jones looked doubtful. He turned to their guide. 'Is that all right with you, Mrs Kane?'

'Oh, very well,' sighed Mrs Kane. 'I know that Professor Pond is interested in this sort of nonsense. But please be quick about it. We must get on with our tour.'

The professor turned to Belinda. 'When you said that you could see two ghosts – you didn't mean us, did you, myself and Ms Day?'

'No,' snapped Belinda. 'Don't be so silly! I was pointing at those two behind you – in the funny clothes.'

Mandy and the professor looked round. There was nobody there.

'What a rude child!' exclaimed Mrs Kane. 'This is quite ridiculous! We really must get on and stop wasting our time.'

Mr Jones opened his mouth to scold Belinda, but Professor Pond held up his hand.

'Who do you see, Belinda?'

'I told you – a man and a girl. The girl has long red hair.'

'Counts me out, then,' murmured Mandy, whose hair was short and brown and curly.

'Are they dressed like those people in the portraits on the wall?' asked the professor.

Fitzwizo and Fenella felt most uncomfortable as Belinda's sharp blue eyes swivelled from them to the elaborate Elizabethan clothes in the portraits and back again.

'No, they look different. The girl's wearing a long brown dress. It's very plain.' (Fenella had worn her oldest and plainest dress for *Operation Phantom*. She was, after all, on duty.) 'It hasn't got one of those ruff things round the neck – or puffed sleeves, or anything fancy. She's got nothing on her head. She looks very cross.'

Fenella *was* cross. She had never been *seen* before and she did not like it. It was very rude of this child to stare at her like that – especially when she had not chosen to materialise.

'And the man?' asked Mandy. 'What's he wearing?'

Belinda frowned. 'He doesn't look like those pictures either. He's wearing a funny sort of tunic thing.'

Fitzwizo was not best pleased. There was nothing *funny* about his precious coat of chain mail. He glared at Belinda.

'Aaagh!' she shrieked, clutching at Mr Jones. 'He's got a very nasty face! He's horrible!'

'Don't be so silly, Belinda,' scolded Mr Jones. 'You must stop this nonsense at once!'

Fitzwizo felt quite pleased with himself. His anger never had this effect on his own children. He tried another, fiercer glare. Belinda's shrieks grew louder.

'Call in the ghostbusters!' yelled one of the boys excitedly. 'Call in the ghostbusters! It's just like that film on the telly, Mr Jones!'

Other children joined in with enthusiasm.

'Darren's right, Mr Jones! The one where the

ghostbusters come and spray...'

'And the eyes in the picture begin to...'

'Aaaagh!' shrieked a small girl. 'That picture! Over there! The eyes just started to...'

'That's enough, 5J!' shouted Mr Jones. His face was red with anger. 'In all my years as a teacher I have never, ever, seen such bad behaviour!'

'And nor have I,' declared Mrs Kane, 'in all my years as a guide.'

'I'm so sorry, Mrs Kane,' said Mr Jones. 'And I really must apologise to you, Professor Pond, and to...'

'Just one more question,' interrupted the professor. 'What was so strange about the man's tunic, Belinda?'

'Don't know,' said Belinda sulkily. 'Don't care! Nobody believes me, anyway.'

'Answer the question,' ordered Mr Jones.

'It's all made up of...sort of...links,' mumbled Belinda, 'like chains.'

'A coat of chain mail!' snorted Mrs Kane. 'From the Middle Ages – long before the Elizabethans. That proves it! She's not looking at any Elizabethan ghost. She's making it all up.'

'I'm not!' yelled Belinda. 'I'm *not* making it all up! I don't care if they are middle-aged. I can still see them.'

'I said *from the Middle Ages*, Belinda – not *middle-aged*,' Mrs Kane corrected her. 'Not, of course, that I believe one word of this nonsense.'

'It's not nons...'

'That's enough!' snapped Mr Jones. 'I don't want to

hear another word from you, Belinda Smith.'

'She *must* have been making it up,' said Mandy, as she and the professor followed the school party up the wide stone stairs. 'Those clothes were all wrong.'

'That's just what puzzles me,' said Professor Pond, frowning. 'If she was making it all up, why *didn't* she make her ghosts look like the portraits? It doesn't make sense.' He tapped the large camera slung around his neck. 'If that child *sees* anything else, I'll try to take some photographs. There may be more to this than meets the eye – our eyes, anyway.'

Four

'Oh, dear!' sighed Fenella, as they trailed along behind Mandy and the professor. 'We've been *seen* on our very first assignment. Not a good start for *Operation Phantom.*'

Fitzwizo was not discouraged. 'Don't worry, Fen. No one believes her. Things always go wrong at the beginning of these operations. Remember that episode of…?'

'Not now!' groaned Fenella. 'You're talking about TV, Dad. This is *real life*!'

'The Long Gallery,' Mrs Kane was saying, 'runs the full length of Dingley Hall.'

Fenella gasped. Never, ever, had she seen such a beautiful room – so long and light, so richly furnished with tapestries, statues, portraits.

'This,' continued their guide, 'is a very famous portrait of the Earl and Countess of Middleshire, who built

23

Dingley Hall. And this,' she turned to the portrait of a young boy, posing stiffly in doublet and hose, 'is their only son, Richard. You can see that he's wearing...'

'You don't have to look at the painting,' Fitzwizo nudged Fenella. 'There's the real thing. There's Richard – over there!'

Fenella stared. Her father was right. The young Elizabethan boy, standing in front of the huge marble fireplace, looked as if he had just stepped out of his own portrait. He was wearing the same bright blue doublet and hose, the same white ruff around his neck. He was gazing eagerly, longingly, at the party of schoolchildren.

'He doesn't know we can see him,' whispered Fitzwizo.

'He wouldn't care about us, anyway, Dad. He's only interested in the children. He'd love to make friends with them.'

'Now's his chance! Look, Fen! Belinda's just spotted him.'

Sure enough, Belinda (the child with the *seeing* eyes) kept glancing towards the fireplace.

'She can see us, too,' said Fenella. 'But she's not saying anything. She doesn't want to get into any more trouble.'

'Pay attention, Belinda!' scolded Mr Jones. 'Mrs Kane is going to tell us all about this famous tapestry.'

Richard, still thinking that he was invisible, had decided to have a bit of fun. He suddenly started dancing about, waggling his fingers on his ears and pulling silly faces at the children of 5J.

This was too much for Belinda. She stared directly at Richard and made some pretty horrible faces of her own.

Richard stopped dead in his tracks, mouth open in amazement. This child couldn't possibly *see* him! In hundreds of years, such a thing had never happened. No, she must be making faces at thin air – for her own amusement.

Just to make sure, he stuck his tongue out at Belinda. Immediately, she did the same back. He waggled his fingers on his ears again. So did she.

'Belinda!' Mr Jones was horrified. 'Stop that at once!'

'*He's* doing it!' cried Belinda, pointing towards the fireplace. '*He* started it!'

'Who?' asked Mandy, while Professor Pond quickly took some photographs of the fireplace. 'Who do you see, Belinda?'

'That boy, the one from the picture – Richard. He's very rude. He keeps making horrible faces and sticking out his tongue.'

They all stared at the young boy in the portrait, looking so serious and proud. Then they stared at the empty marble fireplace.

'Don't be so silly!' snapped Mrs Kane. 'There's nothing there. And a noble Elizabethan child would *never* behave in such a manner.'

'I wouldn't be too sure of that,' chuckled Fitzwizo. 'Noble children from the Middle Ages were none too perfect either – eh, Fen?'

Fenella did not reply.

Young Richard was getting more and more excited. He now knew that Belinda really *could* see him. He could play with this child. He had a friend. His eyes danced with mischief as he hopped around.

'Catch me if you can!' he chanted, racing off down the Long Gallery. 'Catch me if you can!'

No one, apart from Belinda, Fitzwizo and Fenella, could see Richard or hear his merry chant.

'I can catch you – easy peasy!' cried Belinda, chasing after him.

'Quick Mandy, switch on your recorder,' whispered the professor.

Mandy took a small but powerful sound recorder from her handbag and switched it on.

'*BELINDA SMITH!*' shouted Mr Jones. 'Come back here at once!'

'Call in the ghostbusters!' yelled Darren, jumping up and down with excitement. 'What did I tell you, Mr Jones? You need the ghostbusters!'

Like wildfire, the excitement spread. Noisily, 5J started chasing Belinda and each other up and down the full length of the Long Gallery. They could not see or hear the young Elizabethan boy who was dodging happily in and out among them. Those who felt a sudden, sharp, tickling sensation in the stomach did not know that Richard had just raced straight through them.

'That's cheating!' gasped Belinda, puffing along behind him. 'I can't do that. I can't run *through* people.'

Richard didn't care. He hadn't had so much fun for

centuries. It reminded him of birthday parties in the old days. Then, as now, the Long Gallery had been full of noisy, laughing children instead of solemn visitors. And in the evening, for the grown-ups, there had been music and singing and dancing.

It was all too much for Mrs Kane. She sank down on to one of the heavy, carved Elizabethan chairs.

'You're not supposed to sit on that, Mrs Kane,' a small girl protested sharply. 'You told us so.'

'Go away, little girl!' hissed Mrs Kane. 'I don't care what I told you. *JUST – GO – AWAY!*'

By this time Mr Jones had managed to grab Belinda by the arm. He held on to her firmly as he gathered his class around him. The children had never seen him look so angry.

'You have behaved *disgracefully* today, 5J. I am thoroughly ashamed of you – especially of one *very, very* silly child.' He glared at Belinda. 'You must apologise at once to Mrs Kane, Ms Day and Professor Pond. I'm sure that your behaviour, Belinda Smith, has completely spoilt this tour for all of them.'

'Not at all, Mr Jones,' said Professor Pond. 'I have found it all most interesting – very interesting indeed.'

Mrs Kane stood up rather shakily and looked at her watch. Her face brightened. 'I'm afraid your time is up, Mr Jones.' She gave Belinda a very nasty look. 'I know that *one* of your pupils has done her very best to ruin this visit. But I do hope, children, that you have learnt *something* about the Elizabethans.'

'It was great, Mrs Kane,' chirped Darren. 'I thought it was going to be dead boring.'

The rest of the class agreed enthusiastically.

'Better than the Adventure Park!'

''specially when Belinda saw...'

'The eyes in that picture really did...'

'Yeah! I were dead scared when...'

'That's enough, 5J,' Mr Jones interrupted hastily, as Mrs Kane sank back on to the forbidden Elizabethan chair. 'We've got to hurry or we'll be late for the school bus. Say thank you to Mrs Kane, children.'

'Thank you, Mrs Kane,' chanted 5J.

Mrs Kane said nothing. She was beyond speech.

Still chattering excitedly, the school party made its noisy way out of the room. Young Richard, unwilling to let them go, trailed along behind. When they had gone, the Long Gallery seemed very, very quiet.

Professor Pond cleared his throat. 'Thank you, Mrs Kane. That was a very...er...interesting afternoon. Ms Day and I have been given permission to use the kitchen as the base for our overnight stay. We'll make our way along there now, if that's all right with you.'

Still speechless, Mrs Kane nodded dumbly.

'I wonder,' said Fitzwizo, 'if we'll see our young friend again – or anyone else.'

'We won't see Richard again,' said Fenella firmly. 'That's for sure. He's only interested in the children. Other visitors are boring.'

28

She was right. They did not see Richard again, or any of the other inhabitants of Dingley Hall – if there were any.

Nor, in spite of all their overnight investigations, did Professor Pond or Mandy find any evidence of ghostly activity. With their torches, they explored every single room. They placed thermometers in strategic places, to record any sudden falls in temperature. They took more photographs, made more sound recordings. But, to their great disappointment, they saw nothing – heard nothing.

'Oh, dear!' sighed Fitzwizo, as he settled himself into Professor Pond's car next morning. 'I don't know how to tell your mother that we've been *seen*, Fen.'

'Perhaps we shouldn't mention that part of it, Dad. You know how she worries.'

'You're right, Fen. Best not to worry her.'

They told Lady Marigold all about Dingley Hall – well, almost all. They did not tell her about the child with the *seeing* eyes. Fenella described the furniture, the portraits, the statues and the large and beautiful windows with their diamond-shaped panes of glass.

'And all after our time,' sighed her mother. 'It sounds so lovely and so comfortable. Doesn't it, Percy?'

Percival was not impressed. 'It's all right, I suppose, but it is only a house after all – not a great castle like Coldhill.'

'It sounds much more attractive than anything in that

29

dreadful modern town of yours, Frederick,' said Lady Marigold.

'It was very nice, Marigold,' agreed her husband, 'very nice indeed. But still a bit old-fashioned for my taste – no television, no computers, no …'

'Never mind all that,' snapped Percival. 'What matters is whether Dingley Hall will get any phantoms. Did those Ofspook people see anything unusual?'

'No,' Fitzwizo replied truthfully, 'Professor Pond and Mandy didn't see any ghosts.'

'You know, Dad,' said Fenella, when she and her father were alone, 'that Belinda wasn't a very nice child, but she *was* telling the truth. I feel really sorry for her.'

'She was our enemy,' said Fitzwizo sternly. '*Never* feel sorry for your enemy. That is one of the first lessons I had to learn as a young knight. All's fair in love and war – and this is *war*, Fenella.'

Five

When Ms Grimwood marched into the office on Friday, Fitzwizo and Fenella were already there.

'Stupid heating system!' fumed Ms Grimwood, fiddling with the control knob on the radiator. '*Nothing* in this place seems to work efficiently.'

'It's that office ghost again!' laughed Mandy, as she and Professor Pond came into the room. 'This building is haunted. That's why the temperature keeps dropping.'

Ms Grimwood gave her a cold stare. 'Haunted, Ms Day? A modern office block? What nonsense!'

'Mandy was only joking,' protested Professor Pond.

'We do not joke in this office,' barked Ms Grimwood. 'If you have no objection, Ms Day, we must get down to work at once.'

'Silly old bag!' muttered Fenella. (Just as well that she could not be heard!)

'Fenella!' scolded her father. 'Your mother would be shocked to hear such language.' (Fitzwizo himself was not so shocked. He'd heard a lot worse on TV!)

'I am assuming,' continued Ms Grimwood, 'that you followed the Ofspook guidelines in your investigation of Dingley Hall. Do you feel that it merits one or more phantoms in any of the three categories – ghostly sounds, sightings, atmosphere?'

Professor Pond hesitated. 'Well – we ourselves did not observe any ghostly activity. But some very strange events did occur during our visit.'

'There was this child,' said Mandy, 'and she saw…'

'If you don't mind,' snapped Ms Grimwood, 'I would prefer to hear Professor Pond's account of the investigation.'

'Mandy is right,' said Professor Pond. 'We *have* to tell you what this schoolchild saw and heard. The more I think about it, the more convinced I am that she was telling the truth.'

Ms Grimwood sighed. 'Very well, Professor Pond. I'm listening.'

'Oh, no!' groaned Fitzwizo. 'That Belinda will get lots of phantoms for them. I told you she was our enemy, Fen.'

'Don't worry, Dad. Look at old Grimwood's face. She doesn't believe a word of it.'

Fenella was right. Ms Grimwood's mouth tightened as the professor told her all about the child with the *seeing* eyes.

'I have *never,*' she declared, when he had finished,

'heard such utter nonsense! I wanted a proper scientific investigation, Professor Pond. Surely you cannot expect to award Ofspook phantoms on the word of some silly schoolgirl!'

'It's not *just* her word,' protested Mandy. 'The photographs don't show anything, but I'm sure this is young Richard's voice on the sound recorder. Listen!'

The loudest voice on the recording was that of Mr Jones, shouting at Belinda and scolding 5J. They could hear the children running around, laughing and calling to each other. Then, high and clear, a young boy's voice chanted, 'Catch me if you can! Catch me if you can!'

'That's Richard!' exclaimed Mandy, switching off the recorder. 'I'm sure of it. This recorder can pick up sounds, like ghost voices, that can't be heard by the human ear.'

'Really?' sniffed Miss Grimwood. 'To me, that sounded like a class of *very* badly behaved school-children. Any one of them could have been using those words. This proves *nothing*.'

'There!' said Fenella, nudging her father. 'What did I tell you? I knew she wouldn't believe them.'

'I'm afraid that I cannot agree with you, Ms Grimwood,' said Professor Pond. 'During my time at Middleshire University, I did quite a lot of research into these matters.'

'You,' sneered Ms Grimwood, 'are a retired university professor. Some of your views might be considered a little old-fashioned – rather out of date.'

'So are ghosts,' muttered Mandy under her breath.

'What was that, Ms Day? Did you say something?'

'No, Ms Grimwood.'

'Good! I was afraid that it might be another of your little jokes. As for Dingley Hall, I shall allow *one* phantom for atmosphere. That is all.'

'Only one phantom!' chortled Fitzwizo. 'I think we'll be able to beat that, Fen. Don't you?'

'I hope so, Dad. You don't think we could ever get the top score – five starred phantoms?'

'No,' admitted Fitzwizo, 'not really. But we can always try, Fen. There's no harm in reaching for the moon.'

'Or even the stars, Dad.'

'Or even the stars,' chuckled Fitzwizo. 'You and Mandy would get on well, Fen – with your little jokes.'

Fenella sighed. Her father was right. Mandy was just the sort of friend that she would like to have. If only...

'Come on, Fen! Back to base! We must prepare for our Ofspook inspection. There's a lot of work to be done.'

Back at Coldhill Castle, Fitzwizo gathered his family around him.

'Now,' he announced importantly, 'we will have what the police call a briefing session. I am reporting on the Ofspook meeting which took place at 0900 hours on...'

'We know all that,' interrupted Percival. 'Just get on with it, Father!'

Fitzwizo ignored him. Percival had never watched

television. He knew nothing about these matters.

'I'm so pleased,' said Lady Marigold, when Fitzwizo had finished his briefing, 'that Dingley Hall only got one phantom. That's good news, isn't it, Frederick?'

'So far, so good,' agreed Fitzwizo. 'But it is only one site, Marigold. Some others are sure to do much better. Here at Coldhill Castle we must aim for...*what was that?*'

A blood-curdling scream, echoing around the castle walls, had made them all jump – all except Lady Marigold.

'Just practising,' she said sweetly. 'How was that, dear?'

'Terrible,' said her husband. 'I mean, very good. But don't do it again without warning us, Marigold.'

'You might scare us all to death, Mum,' chuckled Fenella.

'Ha! Ha! Very funny,' sneered Percival. Unlike Mandy, he was not fond of a little joke.

'I *am* rather proud of my scream,' admitted Lady Marigold. 'I haven't done one like that for well over a hundred years. Do you remember, dear, when we wanted to frighten...?'

'We really must get on with the meeting, Marigold. I want you all to think carefully about the three categories – sightings, sounds, atmosphere.'

'I could materialise in my suit of armour,' suggested Percival. 'In fact, I'm wearing some of it now.'

'As if we hadn't noticed,' groaned Fenella.

Percival ignored her. 'I'll just go and finish putting it

35

on. When I come back, you must imagine that you've never seen me in full armour before.'

'That won't be easy,' Fenella pointed out. 'Not when you've been clomping around in it, or bits of it, for hundreds of years.'

'I think it's an excellent idea, Percy,' said Fitzwizo. 'Just the sort of thing to impress Ofspook.'

When Percival returned, even Fenella had to admit that he did look impressive. His highly polished armour gleamed in the sunlight as he paced stiffly towards them. Then –

CRASH! BANG! CLANG!

The noble knight had tripped over a loose stone and lay stretched flat out on the castle floor.

'Percy!' wailed Lady Marigold, as they all rushed over to him. 'Are you all right? Are you hurt? Percy, speak to me!'

Percival's visor had snapped shut. A strangled sort of moaning sound came from inside his helmet.

'Now that's an interesting sound,' said Fitzwizo enthusiastically. 'That might impress...'

'Frederick!' scolded Lady Marigold. 'How *could* you think of such a thing! Percy may be badly hurt. We must get his helmet off at once. Fenella, you can undo the breastplate.'

When Percival finally struggled to his feet, Fenella could see that his pride was hurt more than anything else.

'Stop fussing, Mother!' he snapped. 'I'm fine.'

'I still think that appearing in full armour is a good

idea, Percy,' said Fitzwizo. 'But I don't think you should walk about in it. Get into position. Stand still – and *then* materialise.'

'Your father's right,' said Lady Marigold. 'Then you won't fall over, dear.'

'Don't go on about it, Mother,' growled Percival. 'I have *never* fallen over before.'

'Mind you,' said Fenella, 'all that crashing and clanging might go down well under *ghostly sounds*. Perhaps you should make it part of your act, Percy.'

'Very funny! If you're so clever, let's see what you can do.'

'I don't know,' admitted Fenella. 'I'll have to think about it.'

'I could always float through a wall or two,' offered Lady Marigold. 'That usually goes down well. In fact, it's what I'm best at – *watch*!'

Slowly, dreamily, she floated off through the thick castle wall and back again. 'Will that do, Frederick?'

'Yes, dear. That's perfect.'

'I suppose I could walk about in my best blue velvet gown and tall hat, carrying a candle,' suggested Fenella.

'Now that's what I call *really* exciting,' sneered Percival.

'Don't be so unkind, Percy,' scolded his mother. 'I think that's a lovely idea. We so seldom see you in your best clothes, Fenella.'

'Very suitable,' agreed Fitzwizo. 'Well, that about wraps it up for now, team. I think we've made a good start on *Operation Phantom.*'

'But what about you, Father?' asked Percival. 'What are you going to do?'

Fitzwizo frowned. 'I shall have to give the matter some thought, Percy. So far, I've been much too busy to think about it. I have had to organise, take decisions, make plans.'

'Be careful, Dad!' warned Fenella. 'For a moment there, you sounded just like Ms Grimwood.'

'Did I?' Fitzwizo looked rather pleased. 'Well, I suppose I am a bit of a manager myself. We knights had a lot of organising to do in the old days, you know. Have I told you about…?'

'I'm sure you have, Father,' groaned Percival. 'But can we *please* get back to the present? You were talking about plans.'

'I have not forgotten that, Percival,' said Fitzwizo crossly. 'If you had not interrupted, I was about to point out that *Operation Phantom* is our own, modern battle plan.'

'Since no other ghosts know about Ofspook,' said Percival, 'we must have an excellent chance of beating them.'

'It doesn't seem quite fair,' said Fenella. 'The others know nothing about the *Good Ghost Guide* either. I feel as if we're cheating.'

'Don't be so silly, Fen!' snapped Percival. 'We want to get more phantoms than anyone else in that book. All's fair in love and war – especially when the future of Coldhill Castle is at stake.'

'Percy is right,' said Fitzwizo approvingly. (He didn't often approve of his son!) 'As I told you, Fen, *never* feel sorry for the enemy. Percy has remembered what he learnt at Knight School. In the old days, Fenella, your brother would have made a very good knight.'

'I'll say goodnight as well.' Lady Marigold, who had not really been listening, yawned widely. She drifted towards the wall. 'Are you coming, Frederick? You mustn't work too late, dear. You're not getting any younger, you know.'

'Just coming, Marigold.'

'It's been a busy day,' said Fenella. 'I bet you feel dead tired, Dad.'

'No,' said Fitzwizo, 'I don't.'

And he didn't. He didn't feel dead anything. There were tactics to be worked out, plans to be made. He hadn't felt so alive since – well, since he'd been alive!

Six

'This is quite ridiculous!' Ms Grimwood was shouting, as Fitzwizo and Fenella drifted into the office on Monday morning. 'I have read your report on Dingley Hall, Professor Pond. You cannot possibly include the ravings of a silly schoolgirl!'

As I said before, Professor Pond was a gentle man. He did not like anger. But he was also the sort of man who would not give in – not if he thought he was right.

'I'm afraid that I must insist, Ms Grimwood,' he said firmly. 'I have accepted your decision to give Dingley Hall only one phantom. But, in my opinion, what Belinda claimed to have seen and heard is of some importance. It must be mentioned. I shall make it perfectly clear that Mandy and I saw and heard nothing.'

'We saw and heard Belinda,' said Mandy. 'I agree with Professor Pond. It must be included. After all, what harm can it do?'

'*Harm*!' Ms Grimwood spun round and faced Mandy.

Her green eyes blazed with anger. 'We are going to look like complete fools, Ms Day, when that report goes to Ofspook headquarters. This department – *my* department – will be a laughing stock. *That* is the sort of harm it will do.'

'Does that matter,' asked Professor Pond, 'as long as we're telling the truth?'

'Very well!' Ms Grimwood marched over to her desk and sat down abruptly. 'You may write your report, Professor Pond, as you wish. I shall send a covering letter to Mr Grey, the director of Ofspook. I shall make my own views on the matter quite clear. As your head of department, I carry no responsibility for this stupid report. Is that understood?'

'Perfectly,' said Professor Pond.

'Tomorrow,' added Ms Grimwood, 'you are going to visit Midwick Castle. Do remember that, this time, I expect a proper scientific investigation. I do not want second-hand stories about ghosts who run around and make silly faces.'

'But,' protested Mandy, 'we had to tell you what...'

'That is enough, Ms Day! There is work to be done. While you were away, I started to establish computer files on all the places to be visited – history, any previous sightings and so forth. I am taking them in alphabetical order and have just completed the file on Coldhill Castle. I would like you to continue with this work. You do know how to establish computer files, Ms Day?'

'Mandy is something of an expert,' said Professor Pond. 'She knows much more about computers than I do.'

'That,' sneered Ms Grimwood, 'does not make her an expert. I think you'll both find that *I* am the computer expert around here.'

'I do know how to establish files,' said Mandy. Fenella could see that she was cross and upset.

'Poor Mandy, Dad! That old bag really has it in for her.'

Fitzwizo was not listening. He was muttering excitedly to himself. Here and there Fenella picked up the word *computer*.

'What are you on about, Dad?'

'Just think!' Fitzwizo cried suddenly, making Fenella jump. 'Just think, Fen! We, the Fitzwizos, are on the computer! Coldhill Castle is on the computer! We have our *very own file*!'

Fenella felt a bit embarrassed by her father's enthusiasm. She was very glad that no one else could hear him or see him.

'Wouldn't you just *love* to see our file, Fen? To see our names on the computer?'

'I suppose so, Dad. But what's stopping us?'

Fitzwizo sighed. 'We're *ghosts*, Fen! That's what's stopping us. Ghosts can't use computers.'

'I don't see why not. Anyway, you and I are not like other ghosts, Dad. I know that Mum doesn't like to admit it, but we *are* descended from the old Fitzwizo wizards. We have special powers – remember?'

'Not *that* special! No Fitzwizo has ever been known to use a computer.'

'Of *course* they haven't, Dad. There were no computers in the days of the old Fitzwizo wizards. They didn't travel in buses or cars either, did they? Who says we can't use a computer? We've never tried.'

'You know, Fen,' said her father admiringly, 'you really are a very clever girl. I would never have thought of all that. You're right, of course. We've never tried.'

'Come on!' urged Fenella, when the others had gone for lunch. 'Now's our chance, Dad! I'm not saying we *can* use the computers – but we might as well have a go.'

Fitzwizo hesitated. 'This may not be such a good idea, Fen. They don't take much time for lunch. What if…?'

Fenella ignored him. She sat down in Mandy's chair and faced the computer. Fitzwizo hovered anxiously behind her.

'You have to use that plastic thing, Fen. It's called a mouse.'

'*I know, Dad. I know*. I've been watching them for years. I know exactly what to do.'

Fenella clicked the mouse. The screen filled up with little boxes, menus.

'It's working!' Her father hopped about excitedly. 'The Fitzwizo wizards have done it again! You're a… what do they call them? A computer whizkid, Fen – a wizokid- a Fitzwizokid!'

'Calm down, Dad! I'm trying to concentrate. Go and use one of the other computers. Use Ms Grimwood's.'

Fitzwizo shuddered. 'Not on your life! I'll try the professor's machine.'

Fitzwizo was in his seventh heaven. He had always been fascinated by computers, ever since they were first invented. But never, even in his wildest dreams, had he ever imagined that he himself could use one. 'Look!' he cried, clicking his mouse enthusiastically. 'There we are, Fen! In that little box – *Coldhill Castle*!'

'Yes, Dad. I can see it.'

Fitzwizo moved the cursor to the Coldhill Castle box and clicked again. The screen filled up with writing about his ancestral home.

'I like this bit, Fen. Listen! – *In its heyday this was a very important medieval castle. Its position was...*'

But Fenella wasn't listening. She glanced quickly over at her father. He was absorbed in his reading. That should give her just enough time...

'Have you read this, Fen? *For many years the castle was home to the distinguished Fitzwizo family*. Your mother would like that, Fen – *distinguished*.'

'Quick! There's someone coming, Dad.'

There was just enough time to clear their screens before Ms Grimood strode into the office. She saw and heard nothing.

'Phew! That was close, Fen. I didn't quite get to the end of our file. Did you?'

'No, Dad. I didn't.'

Fenella did not tell her father that she hadn't even *started* to read their file. The writing on her screen had *not* been about Coldhill Castle.

'Dad, why don't we go home now and have another practice?'

Fitzwizo looked at her in surprise. 'You're not usually so keen to get home. What's the hurry, Fen?'

Fenella did not tell him – not the real reason, anyway.

'They could come to Coldhill Castle at any time, Dad. We'll be away at Midwick Castle all day tomorrow. That doesn't leave much time for practising.'

Fitzwizo frowned. 'You're right, Fen. I didn't see anything on the file about when they were coming to us. Did you?'

'No, Dad, I didn't. Come on! Let's go!'

'Goodness!' exclaimed Professor Pond, when he and Mandy returned to the office. 'It does feel a lot warmer in here.'

'No doubt Ms Day would say that the office ghosts had just left,' sneered Ms Grimwood.

'No, I would not!' Mandy said crossly, sitting down at her desk. 'You know perfectly well that I was only joking.'

She was getting fed up with Ms Grimwood's nasty remarks. No wonder everyone had hated her in her last office! The woman was a bully. She liked to upset people.

A tiny green envelope had appeared in the top, right-hand corner of Mandy's computer screen. That meant that someone had sent her a message. Usually, any message on her computer was about work. Sometimes (and Ms Grimwood knew nothing about this) it was from her boyfriend, Jamie, who worked in a nearby office block. Luckily, her computer faced away from Ms Grimwood.

Mandy moved the cursor up to the envelope and clicked. As the message flashed on to the screen, she frowned. It said:

> *Dear Mandy,*
> *I really like your little jokes. I think you're a great ghosthunter – and I should know! Don't let old Grimwood get you down! From your friend,*
>
> *Fen*

Mandy stared at the screen. Was this Jamie's idea of a joke? If not – who was Fen?

'Ms Day!' Mandy jumped as Ms Grimwood's harsh voice broke in on her thoughts. 'We are not paid to day-dream in this office. Are you getting on with those files?'

'What? Oh…yes, Ms Grimwood.' Hastily, Mandy clicked the mouse. 'I've got as far as the file on Dunstan Abbey. I'm working on that now.'

But Mandy did not find it easy to concentrate on the history of Dunstan Abbey. Jamie *must* have sent that strange message. What other friend knew all about her little jokes, the ghosthunting, Ms Grimwood – *and* knew how to get in touch through her computer?

Seven

Meanwhile, back at the castle, the practice was not going well.

Fenella was pacing up and down in her blue velvet dress and tall conical hat, carrying a candle. Her hat had already fallen off twice and the candle had just tipped out of its holder.

Mandy will have read my message by now, she thought miserably. I shouldn't have done it! I shouldn't! Dad will go mad if he finds out.

'Fenella!' scolded Fitzwizo. 'What *has* got into you? It was your idea to have this practice – remember? There's no time tomorrow, with going to Midwick Castle.'

'Midwick Castle!' exclaimed Lady Marigold. 'Did you say Midwick Castle, Frederick?'

'Yes, we're going there tomorrow.'

'But you might see *them*, Frederick!' (Fitzwizo had never known his wife to get so excited.) 'After all these years you might *see* them again!'

Fitzwizo sighed. What was wrong with everyone today? First Fenella and now Lady Marigold. This practice was not going according to plan.

'What might we see, dear?' he asked patiently.

'Why – our old friends, of course!'

'Our old friends,' Fitzwizo repeated cautiously. 'What old friends?'

Lady Marigold stared at him in disbelief. 'You are going to Midwick Castle, Frederick – home of our oldest and dearest friends, Sir Hugo and Lady Lettice de Vere. You can't have forgotten Hugo and Letty!'

'Of course I haven't forgotten them,' said Fitzwizo hastily. 'It's been a long time, that's all.'

'I do so wish I could come with you,' said Lady Marigold. 'It would be just like old times.'

'You can't travel, Marigold. You haven't got the blood of the old Fitzwizo wizards in your veins.'

Lady Marigold shuddered. 'Please don't talk about that, Frederick. You know it always upsets me. And don't mention it to Letty or Hugo either.'

'We might not even see them,' Fitzwizo pointed out. 'A lot of people must have lived in that castle since their time.'

'Yes,' sighed Lady Marigold, 'I hadn't really thought about that. Anyway, I expect that beautiful castle is just a ruin now, like Coldhill.' She brushed her delicate white hand across her forehead. 'Could we stop practising now, dear? I can feel one of my headaches coming on.'

'We can't stop now!' protested Percival. 'It takes me

49

ages to get into full armour.'

'Your mother's not feeling well, Percy. I'm afraid we'll have to call the practice off for the moment. But,' Fitzwizo added sternly, 'we'll have to work much harder than this if we want to impress Ofspook.'

'I know, dear,' sighed Lady Marigold. 'I'm so sorry. I suppose I'm just not used to all this excitement. You see, the past few centuries have been so very quiet.'

'I do understand that,' said Fitzwizo. 'But we must get down to some really serious work after this visit to Midwick Castle.'

'I'd forgotten that Aunt Letty and Uncle Hugo lived there,' said Fenella. 'And don't worry, Mum. If we see them, we'll give them your love.'

Fenella was not looking forward to the car journey to Midwick Castle. Mandy might talk about the computer message. Fitzwizo would be very angry.

As it happened, she needn't have worried. After his exhausting whirl down the hill, it wasn't long before her father was snoring loudly in the back seat of Professor Pond's car. In any case Mandy did not, even once, mention the mysterious message. It seemed that the professor knew nothing about it.

Fenella felt so relieved that she, too, dozed off. She only woke up when Fitzwizo nudged her. 'This isn't like you, Fen. Wake up! Look!'

They were turning into the car park at Midwick Castle. Fenella rubbed her eyes and stared. Walls and towers, complete and perfect, rose up on the other side of a wide deep moat. *This* was no crumbling ruin. This was like her own home as it used to be – and as she vaguely remembered it, many centuries ago.

Midwick Castle, so different now from Coldhill, was packed with visitors. In each room stood a guide, dressed in medieval clothes. Slowly, Mandy and the professor made their way around. Fitzwizo was filled with envy as he and Fenella followed them.

'You can still walk right round the battlements,' marvelled Fenella. 'We used to be able to do that – remember?'

'I remember,' said her father grimly. 'Money has been spent on this place, Fen. That's what it is – money. Since our time, not a penny has been spent on Coldhill.'

In the Great Hall, they stared at the beamed ceiling, the beautiful tapestries, the long banqueting table. A guide, dressed in tunic and hose, stood by the huge fireplace. He was telling visitors all about the wonderful restoration work carried out by the fifth Duke of Midwick.

'It's not fair!' said Fenella. 'Mum would love all this. She gets so worried about our castle being knocked down.'

'Best not to tell her about it, Fen. No point. It would only...'

'FITZ!' bellowed a hearty voice (heard only by Fenella and her father). 'I don't believe it! Fitz – my old

51

friend! What on earth are you doing here?'

A tall powerfully-built man, in blue tunic and scarlet cloak, came striding towards them. Fenella noticed that some of the visitors gave a sudden shiver as he walked, unseen, right through them.

'Hugo!' Fitzwizo, clasped in a strong bear hug, beamed delightedly. 'Marigold thought we might still find you here.'

Sir Hugo held Fitzwizo at arm's length and looked him up and down. 'It's been a long time, my old friend. You haven't changed a bit. Now, where's Marigold?'

'She wasn't able to come with us. But you remember my daughter, Fenella?'

Fenella gasped for air as she, in her turn, was clasped in Sir Hugo's arms. 'Fenella! Little Fen! Of course I remember you! Do you still have that temper to go with your red hair?'

'No,' said Fenella crossly, 'I do not...' Her voice tailed off as she caught her father's grin. 'Well...just sometimes.'

'Where's Letty?' asked Fitzwizo.

'She's in the West Tower. It's out of bounds to visitors while they repair the stairs. She'll be so surprised to see you. Come on!'

Lady Lettice, sitting quietly in the window seat with her needlework, was more than surprised to see them. She sprang to her feet, dropping her embroidery, and stared in disbelief.

Short and plump, in her green dress, she was just as Fenella remembered her. At this moment her face was as white as the wimple that covered her hair.

'You look as if you'd just seen a ghost, Letty,' joked her husband. He dug Fitzwizo in the ribs. 'Get it, Fitz? *Just seen a ghost*. That's a good one – eh?'

'Yes,' said Fitzwizo, remembering how keen his old friend was on jokes and pranks, 'very good.'

'Well, Letty,' demanded Sir Hugo, 'aren't you pleased to see old Fitz again? And I'm sure you haven't forgotten Fenella, our naughty little redhead?'

Fenella scowled at him. What age did he think she was?

Lady Lettice had recovered by now. The colour had returned to her normally rosy cheeks. She stepped forward and hugged Fitzwizo and Fenella.

'When we last saw Fenella,' she reminded her husband, 'she was a tall young lady – just as she is now. She was no longer a naughty child, Hugo.'

Fenella liked Lady Lettice. She remembered that she had always liked her mother's friend. It was all coming back to her.

'But why hasn't Marigold come with you?' asked Lady Lettice. 'It would be lovely to see her, after all these years. She was my dearest friend, you know.'

'I know,' said Fitzwizo. 'She did want to come but…'

'How did *you* manage to come?' demanded Sir Hugo. 'That's what I'd like to know. We can't ever leave Midwick Castle. So how can you two leave Coldhill?'

'Well,' Fitzwizo tried desperately to think of an

explanation, 'we…that is, Fen and myself…we can…'

'I expect,' Lady Lettice interrupted gently, 'that it's all down to those old Fitzwizo wizards.'

'You knew!' exclaimed Fitzwizo. 'You knew all the time about the wizardly blood in our veins! You never said.'

'No,' said Lady Lettice. 'We guessed that Marigold wasn't very happy about it. We didn't want to upset her.'

'You know, I'd forgotten all about that,' said Sir Hugo. 'But talking of Coldhill – how is the old place? Has the castle changed at all?'

Fitzwizo looked around the tower room. A tapestry, showing a hunting scene, hung on the freshly plastered wall. Cosy rush matting covered the floor. He thought of his own cold stone floors and crumbling walls. What could he say?

'Hasn't changed a bit,' Fenella said firmly, as her father hesitated. 'It's just as you both remember it. Isn't it, Dad?'

Fitzwizo looked gratefully at his daughter. She was right, of course. Neither of them wanted to lie – but they couldn't possibly tell the truth. Marigold would be so ashamed.

'Yes,' he agreed. 'As Fen says, the old place hasn't changed – not much, anyway.'

'I am glad,' said Lady Lettice. 'I would so much like to see Coldhill Castle again.'

Thank goodness you can't, thought Fenella. She did not feel proud of herself.

'I say!' boomed Sir Hugo. 'Did you two realise that you were standing behind a couple of ghosthunters?'

Fitzwizo jumped. 'Did you say ghosthunters, Hugo? Where? Are you sure?'

'Of course I'm sure. I heard them talking earlier, before I spotted you. They're staying the night, silly things – investigating ghostly activity.'

'We get lots of them here,' said Lady Lettice. 'Hugo and I keep well out of their way.'

'Good idea!' agreed Fitzwizo. 'We like to do the same. Don't we, Fen?'

'Oh, yes – we never have anything to do with people like that. Ghosthunters give me the creeps. They're really spooky.'

Lady Lettice laughed. 'Did you hear that, Hugo? Fenella thinks that ghosthunters are spooky.'

Sir Hugo wasn't listening. He was pacing excitedly up and down the room. Fitzwizo watched him nervously. He knew his friend of old. He was up to something.

'Ha!' barked Sir Hugo, making them all jump. 'Ghostly activity indeed! We'll give them ghosts! We'll give them activity! Now that you're here, Fitz, we might as well have some sport with these ghosthunters. What do you say?'

'Er...well...yes,' gulped Fitzwizo.

He and Fenella looked at each other helplessly. This was just what they *didn't* want. But what could they do? What could they say?

Eight

Midwick Castle was very quiet when all the visitors had gone. Only the guides remained, looking very much at home in their medieval clothes.

'I don't understand why some of the guides are still here,' said Professor Pond, as he and Mandy went from room to room, making notes. He looked at his watch. 'Surely they should be off duty by now.'

'Have you noticed,' whispered Mandy, 'that we keep on seeing the same four people? I don't remember seeing any of those guides during the day.' (Not surprising – since, as you've probably guessed, these 'guides' were really Fitzwizo, Fenella and their two old friends.)

Professor Pond stared at the tall, dark, bearded man who stood by the window, looking out. He was dressed in a fine blue tunic, trimmed with gold – a red cloak slung back over his powerful shoulders.

'Excuse me,' said the professor, walking towards him,

'do you usually work so…?'

But the tall man was no longer there. There was no one standing by the window.

'Can I help you, sir?' asked a soft voice.

Professor Pond spun round to face a short plump guide in a green gown and white wimple.

'We were wondering,' said Mandy, as the professor recovered himself, 'if you always have to work so late.'

'Oh, yes,' said the woman with a smile, 'we're always here long after the visitors have gone.'

'May I take a photograph of you?' asked the professor. 'In that costume, you look as if you've just stepped out of the Middle Ages.'

'You never know!' laughed the guide. 'Perhaps I have!'

The professor raised his camera to his eye. But what he saw was not the rosy-cheeked woman in her green dress and white wimple. He was looking at a neatly framed view of a bare, boring medieval wall.

'She's gone!' said Mandy. 'She just vanished!'

'So did the man by the window! You know, Mandy, I think the ghosts of Midwick Castle are playing tricks on us. Did you manage to record her voice?'

'No, I thought she was a real guide at first so I didn't bother.'

'Never mind. I'm sure we'll see them again. They look as if they're enjoying themselves.'

'That one doesn't look so happy,' whispered Mandy, as they entered the next room.

She was right. Fitzwizo was not enjoying himself at

all. He stood stiffly in the corner, scowling unhappily, and vanished almost as soon as they spotted him.

Fenella made some equally brief appearances, slouching in and out of rooms in a sulky teenage sort of way.

Sir Hugo noticed none of this. He was having the time of his life – or should I say his *afterlife*? Anyway, whatever, he was having fun.

He appeared at windows, gazing soulfully out over the castle grounds. From time to time he strode swiftly past Mandy and the professor, flinging his scarlet cloak back over his shoulder.

Once, as he strode past, the professor tried to take his photograph. At the click of the camera, Sir Hugo stopped dead in his tracks. He turned round and pointed at them dramatically. Then he chanted loudly,

'I AM HUGO DE VERE,
A KNIGHT YOU SHOULD FEAR!'

Instantly, a soft voice from behind Mandy and the professor sang,

'AND I'M LADY LETTICE,
SO GLAD YOU HAVE MET US!'

As they spun round, there was a gentle laugh and a brief glimpse of white wimple and green dress.

'So that guide *was* Lady Lettice!' exclaimed Mandy. 'I thought so. I've been reading all about Lady Lettice and Sir Hugo de Vere. Now I've got both of them on tape – I hope!'

For a while, there were no more glimpses of the 'guides'.

'This is really exciting!' declared Professor Pond. 'In all my years of research, I have never come across such a high level of ghostly activity.'

'You should have brought your spirit level,' joked Mandy. 'Get it? *Spirit level* – to measure the level of ghostly activity!'

Professor Pond laughed. 'I like that, Mandy. Just don't repeat it to Ms Grimwood!'

'You must be joking! I wonder what she'll make of our report on this place!'

'I don't want to think about that – not yet!'

They had reached the Great Hall. No longer crowded with visitors, it seemed very large and very quiet. There were no 'guides' to be seen.

'Perhaps they won't materialise again,' said Mandy.

'They will. Somehow, I don't think we've seen the last of Sir Hugo and friends. They're probably thinking up some other tricks to play on us.'

The professor was right. Sir Hugo had gathered everyone together in the West Tower.

'We certainly put the wind up those ghosthunters!' he chortled. 'This is great sport!'

'I'm so glad you came, Fitz,' said Lady Lettice. 'I haven't enjoyed myself so much for centuries.'

'You just wait!' boomed Sir Hugo. 'It's not over yet!'

'Isn't it?' groaned Fitzwizo, before he could stop himself. 'I mean – haven't we played enough tricks on them?'

'ENOUGH!' roared Sir Hugo. 'We haven't even started yet! What has got into you, old boy? You used to be game for anything.'

'I think Dad's a bit tired after all the travelling,' said Fenella, yawning 'And so am I. Perhaps we should have a rest.'

'Nonsense!' declared Sir Hugo. 'I've got the very thing to liven you both up – a game of Blind Man's Buff! That should get you into the spirit of the thing. *Spirit of the thing* – get it, Fitz?'

Fitzwizo was not laughing. 'Did you say *Blind Man's Buff*?' he asked faintly.

'Yes – in the Great Hall. Don't you remember how we used to love playing it – all the grown-ups and all the children? We'll have another game for old times' sake. We'll amaze these silly ghosthunters!'

Mandy and the professor *were* amazed as the Great Hall suddenly, unbelievably, came to life.

'Quick!' cried the professor. 'Camera! Recorder!'

He and Mandy tried to capture, in sound and film, that incredible game of Blind Man's Buff.

Sir Hugo was, as he had always been, the life and soul of the party. With a great shout, he leapt from floor to table and back again. He balanced on benches, swung from the beams, jumped out from corners – pursued by a blindfolded, giggling Lady Lettice. As she chased frantically after him, the other two trailed reluctantly behind.

'Dad,' whispered Fenella, 'they'll get lots of starred phantoms. We have to stop them – *now*!'

'I know,' sighed Fitzwizo. 'We'll have to tell them the truth, Fen. We've got no choice.'

Lady Lettice, having finally caught her husband, was now busy blindfolding him.

'Hugo,' whispered Fitzwizo, 'can we stop now? I have something very important to tell you.'

'STOP?' roared Sir Hugo. 'But we're having such fun, old boy. We can't stop *now*!'

'Don't be such a spoilsport, Fitz,' cried Lady Lettice. 'Fen always loved Blind Man's Buff. She'll be so disappointed. Won't you, Fen?'

Mandy froze. It was that name again – *Fen*! The message on her computer had come from someone called Fen. It couldn't possibly be…

She stared across the hall – across the centuries – at the tall, red-headed girl in the blue dress. Fenella was standing absolutely still, staring back.

'Fen, what's the matter?' her father asked anxiously.

'You look as pale as a ghost,' laughed Sir Hugo.

'That's not funny,' said Fen. 'Can we stop now, please?'

'But my dears!' exclaimed Lady Lettice, when they were back in the West Tower and Fitzwizo had explained everything. 'Why didn't you tell us all this before?'

'I'm sorry I lied,' Fenella said miserably. 'We just

couldn't tell you the truth about Coldhill Castle. You see, Mum would be so ashamed – especially when *your* castle is so beautiful.'

'I can see why you weren't too keen on all the fun and games, old boy,' said Sir Hugo. 'I was beginning to think you'd turned into a really dull old stick. You were afraid we'd get too many of those starred phantom things, weren't you?'

'Yes,' Fitzwizo confessed. 'I'm sorry. It all sounds so mean – especially when you're both such good friends.'

'I do wish you'd told us, Fitz,' Lady Lettice said gently. 'You see, we don't want any phantoms at all. We have more than enough visitors as it is.'

'We could have had our fun and games,' Sir Hugo added wistfully, 'without materialising in front of those silly Ofspooks or whatever you call them.'

'I know,' sighed Fitzwizo. 'I've been very foolish – very foolish indeed.'

'I can understand why,' said Lady Lettice. 'I'm so sorry to hear about Coldhill Castle. Of course you must get your phantoms – *and* your stars.'

'You wouldn't want to be a starless knight, would you, Fitz?' chortled Sir Hugo. 'Get it? Starless night. Starless...'

'I know!' exclaimed Lady Lettice, ignoring her husband. 'You must make use of your wizardly powers, Fitz. A little bit of magic might help.'

'I can't. Marigold wouldn't like it.'

'The time has come,' Lady Lettice said firmly, 'to tell

Marigold that we know all about the old Fitzwizo wizards – and that it's nothing to be ashamed of. Tell her from me that you must make use of that magic power – for the sake of Coldhill Castle.'

'Aunt Letty is right,' said Fenella. 'And Mum will listen to her. I know she will.'

'Wish I had some wizardly blood in my veins,' Sir Hugo said enviously. 'You're a lucky old ghost, Fitz – able to get out and about like that.'

'You must also use those powers,' Lady Lettice said with a smile, 'to come and visit your old friends again.'

'We will, Aunt Letty,' promised Fenella. 'And we won't leave it for hundreds of years next time.'

Nine

'Do you seriously expect me to believe all this?' demanded Ms Grimwood, when Mandy and the professor had reported back. 'You are telling me that you saw four ghosts who pretended to be guides and made up silly rhymes? Then you saw the same four playing a game of Blind Man's Buff in the Great Hall of Midwick Castle?'

'Yes,' said Professor Pond. 'It was incredible.'

'And you have no evidence of all this – on film or on tape?'

'No. I'm afraid not. The camera didn't pick them up. Nor did the sound recorder. That often happens with ghosts.'

'But we made lots of notes, Ms Grimwood,' said Mandy. 'We wrote it all down.'

'I'm sure you did, Ms Day. And you seriously thought that I would fall for such nonsense?'

'It isn't nonsense!' For once, Professor Pond sounded

really angry. 'We are reporting what we saw and heard. Do you think we're *lying*, Ms Grimwood?'

Ms Grimwood hesitated. 'Not exactly lying, Professor Pond. But I do think that you may have spent too many years on this type of research. It may be that what you saw were not ghosts, but figments of your imagination.'

At the back of the room, Fenella (once more unseen and unheard!) snorted loudly. 'Figments indeed! How dare that stupid woman call us figments – whatever that means!'

'It means,' her father explained, 'that we are imagined – not real.'

'But we *are* real!' protested Fenella. 'We are *real* ghosts!'

'Of course we are, Fen. Don't worry. Ms Grimwood will find that out soon enough. We'll give her figments!'

For Professor Pond and Mandy, the day went from bad to worse.

'I have contacted Head Office,' announced Ms Grimwood. 'As I thought, your findings are quite out of line with all other Ofspook reports. I have been instructed to accompany you on any future visits. It is felt that more common sense and less imagination is required for these investigations. I should tell you that Mr Grey, the director, is not at all happy with your work.'

'We're telling the truth!' Mandy protested angrily. 'I

don't care what the director thinks!'

Ms Grimwood's green eyes glinted coldly. 'You might care, Ms Day, if you were to lose your job in this department.'

'That would be most unfair,' objected Professor Pond. 'Mandy is a very efficient worker.'

Ms Grimwood's icy stare swivelled in his direction. 'It could also be decided, Professor Pond, that you are ready for *full* retirement. It may be that all this research into ghostly activity is not good for your health.'

'I'm not mad, if that's what you mean,' Professor Pond said quietly, 'and nor is Mandy.'

'Well,' sniffed Ms Grimwood, 'as I said, I shall accompany you on all future investigations. Tomorrow I have arranged for us to visit a Victorian town house in Nottingley. It is said to be haunted by the ghost of a young housemaid. But we shall see what we shall see.'

'This time,' Fitzwizo told Fenella, 'we are not going with them. Now that we can use the computers, a change in tactics is called for. We can study the reports as they come in. That will tell us all we need to know.'

'Good thinking, Dad! Anyway, our presence seems to do more harm than good. But you must tell Mum about using some of our wizardly powers.'

'She won't like it,' Fitzwizo said glumly. 'I know she won't.'

Lady Marigold did *not* like it – not one little bit.

'Oh, no!' she moaned. (She was feeling in particularly

low spirits.) 'Not only did you tell Letty and Hugo about the state of Coldhill Castle, but you also had to tell them about those dreadful Fitzwizo wizards. How could you, Frederick?'

'Yes, Father,' Percival said haughtily, 'how could you? Had you forgotten about our family honour?'

'Oh, don't be such a twit, Percy!' snapped Fenella. 'Anyway, they knew already.'

'Did they?' gasped Lady Marigold. 'They never said!'

'Only because they knew you had a thing about it, Mum. *They* never thought it was anything to be ashamed of.'

Fitzwizo chuckled. 'Just the opposite, in fact. Old Hugo wished he had a bit of wizardly power – that he could get out and about like Fen and me.'

'So you see,' said Fenella, 'Aunt Letty is right. Since we've got these magic powers, we might as well make use of them.'

'Well…' Lady Marigold hesitated. 'What do you think, Percy?'

Percival cleared his throat. 'In my opinion,' he declared pompously, 'these powers have always been used very foolishly – for popping in and out of that dreadful town, watching television and so forth. I have no objection if they are used sensibly, for the honour of the Fitzwizos.'

'That's that, then,' said Fitzwizo in his best police inspector tone. 'We must now give all our attention to *Operation Phantom*. There is much work to be done.'

Apart from whirling in and out, (always done where Lady Marigold could not see them) Fenella and her father had never practised any magic within the walls (or what was left of them) of Coldhill Castle.

Now all that had to change. Lady Marigold, supported by Percival, forced herself to watch some of their take-offs and landings. 'Just *watching* you makes me dizzy!' she gasped. 'All that spinning around can't be good for you, Frederick – not at your age.'

'If we get into the *Good Ghost Guide*,' Fenella pointed out, 'there'll be lots of visitors – and lots of buses and cars to take Dad up and down the hill. He won't have to do any more of that whirling.'

'That's true,' Fitzwizo agreed happily. 'And we *will* get into the *Good Ghost Guide,* Fen. We *will* get our visitors. At last, *Operation Phantom* is going according to plan.'

The same could not be said about Ofspook's visit to the Victorian town house in Nottingley.

It was the middle of the night. Ms Grimwood, Professor Pond and Mandy were sitting in the parlour, torches by their sides. 'Just as I thought!' sneered Ms Grimwood. 'No fun and games in this house, Professor – not even in the nursery, where you might expect them!'

'No,' said Professor Pond, 'but the thermometer in this room has registered some sharp falls in temperature.'

'So has the one on the stairs,' said Mandy. 'I felt a strange sort of chill when I last went to check it.'

'Draughts!' Ms Grimwood said scornfully. 'That's all it is – draughts! Victorian houses are full of them.'

In the early morning, no young housemaid came to pull back the curtains and light the fire in the parlour. No children stirred in the night nursery. Apart from the sudden sharp drops in temperature, there was nothing to report.

'We'll give it one phantom for atmosphere,' pronounced Ms Grimwood. 'The director will be most interested to hear about this visit. As I expected, these results are in line with the other Ofspook investigations – no flights of fancy this time!'

A few days later, after office hours, Fitzwizo and Fenella whirled down the hill. They were eager to use the computers again.

'The report on that Victorian house should be finished by now,' said Fitzwizo, as he sat down at Professor Pond's desk. 'We can see what we're up against.'

When Fenella turned on her computer, a small green envelope appeared in the top right-hand corner of the screen. There was a message! It must be for Mandy. It couldn't possibly be for her – or could it? She glanced quickly over at her father. He was busy reading Professor Pond's report. With her mouse, she moved the cursor up to the little green envelope and clicked.

As the message flashed on to the screen, Fenella's stomach turned over with excitement. It *was* for her! It was a message from Mandy – for her!

Fen,
Please tell me who you are. I have not
told anyone about you. This may sound
silly – but did I see you at Midwick
Castle?
PLEASE ANSWER.

        Mandy

'Well,' Fitzwizo chuckled happily, 'that's good news for *Operation Phantom*, isn't it, Fen?'

Fenella jumped. 'Good news? Is it? Why?'

'*Why*?' Fitzwizo stared at her in astonishment. '*Why?* Have you been reading the same report, Fen? Because they didn't see anything. Because the Victorian house only got one phantom for atmosphere. That's why!'

'Oh, yes, I see what you mean, Dad. It is good news for us.'

'Certainly is, Fen. That's one more report we don't have to worry about.'

But Fenella *was* worried. Ms Grimwood would now be sure that Mandy and the professor had been lying in the other reports. The director would think so too. Mandy might lose her job. She might lose it before they even came to Coldhill Castle.

'Could we have another look at our own file, Dad – the one on Coldhill Castle? We hadn't quite finished reading it.'

'Good idea, Fen! We can read it properly this time – no need to rush.'

Fitzwizo was only too pleased to go on using the computer. It was like a wonderful new toy – even better (apart from police programmes) than television. He could take his time. He could read about his ancestral home and his distinguished family all over again. Fenella typed quickly:

> Dear Mandy,
> Yes, you **did** see me at Midwick Castle. I am a ghost, but not (I hope!) a scary one. Don't worry about not seeing anything in the Victorian house. Old Grimwood is enough to spook any ghost – but not me! You won't lose your job. We (I'll explain who later) are on your side. We'll sort out the old battleaxe for you. Got to go now.
> From your friend,
> *Fen*
> P.S. This is our secret.

'Not any more, it isn't!'
Fenella jumped. She had not seen her father standing, very quietly, behind her chair.

Ten

Fitzwizo was not best pleased.

'How long has this been going on?' he demanded. 'How many of these messages have you sent?'

'Only one, Dad, honest! I only wanted to…'

'No excuses!' Fitzwizo interrupted sternly. (He was getting much better at being stern.) 'I would like you to remember, Fenella Fitzwizo, that *I* am in charge of *Operation Phantom*. This was not part of the plan.'

'I know, Dad. I'm sorry. I only wanted to have a friend.'

'A *friend*!' Fitzwizo was astonished. 'We can't make friends with ordinary people. You know that, Fen.'

Fenella was near to tears. 'Why can't we? Who says so?'

'Well…your mother…everybody…that's just the way it is, Fen.'

'I don't believe it! It doesn't *have* to be like that. I know it doesn't!'

Fitzwizo sighed. 'If only Letty and Hugo had a

daughter. You could be friends with her.'

'But don't you see, Dad? That's not what I want. I want a *modern* friend. I can talk properly to Mandy, about music, TV, videos – that sort of thing. You see, Dad, you and I are different. We're not stuck in the Middle Ages, like the others. We've moved on.'

Fitzwizo thought about their visit to Midwick Castle. He could see what Fenella meant. It had been good to see his old friend again but, in so many ways, they were centuries apart. Hugo had never travelled in buses or cars. He had never used a computer or watched TV.

'We don't have to be bound by the old rules, Dad. Anyway, nobody ever said that we ghosts couldn't have a *computer* friend, did they?'

'Don't be silly, Fen. Of course they didn't. There weren't any computers in the old days.'

'There you are, then!' Fenella said triumphantly. 'So I'm not breaking any of the old rules, am I?'

Fitzwizo sighed. 'Oh, all right, Fen. You can have this friendship – as long as it stays on the computer. Make quite sure that it doesn't interfere with *Operation Phantom*. And don't tell your mother about it. You know how she worries.'

Strangely enough, now that Lady Marigold had accepted their magic powers, she seemed to worry much less about everything. Take-offs and landings didn't bother her at all these days.

'I'm glad you're taking it all so lightly, Marigold,'

said Fitzwizo, as his wife came floating gently through the wall. 'You seem quite happy now about the wizardly blood in our veins.'

'Oh, yes, dear,' Lady Marigold said airily. 'Letty was right – as usual. I've been a very silly ghost. You and Fenella have a precious gift. You must use it.'

'It is your *duty* to use it, Father,' declared Percival, 'in order to preserve the ancestral home of the Fitzwizos.'

'And,' muttered Fenella under her breath, 'so that you can show off in your precious suit of armour.'

'When absolutely necessary,' said Fitzwizo in his best police inspector tone, 'we will make use of our special powers in *Operation Phantom*. But we will use them as little as possible. We must remember that we are ghosts these days – ghosts with some wizardly powers, but not full-blooded wizards. And Ofspook is investigating *ghostly activity* – not *magic*.'

Over the next few days, the Fitzwizo family was so busy with *Operation Phantom* that Fenella and her father did not get down to the office. When they did whirl down the hill, after office hours, they found that the Ofspook team had carried out two more investigations.

The first was at an ancient pub called *The Headless Horse*. A white horse, minus its head, was said to gallop noisily around the inn yard at midnight.

'Ugh!' Fenella shuddered. 'I'd hate to see that, Dad! It would scare me to death!'

Anyway, no headless horse had been seen or heard.

Nor had there been any other strange sounds or sightings. The pub had not been awarded *any* phantoms – not even one for atmosphere.

As soon as Fenella reached the end of the report, a little green envelope appeared on the computer screen. When Fenella clicked on to it, there was a message from Mandy.

> *Dear Fen,*
> *You can see what happened at The Headless Horse – nothing! Old Grimwood is now SURE that we were making it all up about Dingley Hall and Midwick Castle. I bet the director will think so too.*
> *I'm afraid we will lose our jobs. You said that you could help us.*
> *We need help – NOW!*
> *Your friend,*
> *   Mandy*

Fenella showed the message to her father. 'We haven't been down to the office for days,' she said miserably. 'Mandy will think I've forgotten all about her.'

They read the second report, about the site of an ancient monastery. Here, at certain times, the monks were said to walk about in procession and chant. They had not chanted for the Ofspook team.

The monastery had been awarded two phantoms. One was for atmosphere and one for the sighting of a solitary monk, pacing about in the ruins of the old chapel. The report stressed that this monk had been seen by Professor Pond and Mandy – not by Ms Grimwood.

On Fenella's computer there was another message from Mandy.

> *Dear Fen,*
> *You did not answer my last message.*
> *Things are **WORSE**. Grimwood does not*
> *believe that we saw the monk. She has told*
> *us to stay at home tomorrow while she has*
> *a meeting in London with the director.*
> ***The meeting is about us.***
> *We think that they will sack us and get a*
> *new team.*
> *If you can – **PLEASE HELP US!***
> *Your friend,*
> *   Mandy*
> *P.S. I will come into the office tomorrow*
> *morning to check for messages.*

Watched by her father, Fenella typed:

> *Dear Mandy,*
> *Just got both your messages. Things are*
> *not looking good. Wait and see what the*
> *old battleaxe has to say. Then we'll think*
> *of a plan.*

DON'T WORRY! WE WILL SAVE YOUR
JOBS!
Your friend,
Fen

'Isn't this a bit foolish, Fen?' asked her father. 'We may not be able to help them.'

'We *have* to help them, Dad. We know they're not lying. And *we're* partly to blame for all this. There wouldn't have been so many sightings if we hadn't been at Dingley Hall and Midwick Castle.'

'I know,' sighed Fitzwizo. 'But don't let any of this interfere with *Operation Phantom*.'

'Don't worry, Dad. I won't.'

Next morning, Fenella could not stop thinking about Mandy. She was really worried about her.

They were not working on *Operation Phantom* until the afternoon. Nobody would notice if she whirled quickly down to the office and back again. Mandy was sure to be there early to check for messages.

Fenella had never gone into town before without her father. Whirling down the hill on her own felt very strange indeed. But what harm could it possibly do? She was only going to check that her computer friend had got her message. Mandy wouldn't even know she was there.

As Fenella had expected, Mandy was in the office before her. She was sitting in front of her computer, staring at the screen. She did not look happy. As Fenella watched, she sighed. Then she started, slowly, to type.

> *Dear Fen,*
> *Got your message. I will let you know what Ms Grimwood says. You are the only one who knows we're not lying. I don't know what you can do to help, but I do need a friend – badly! I just wish that we could…*

Here Mandy stopped typing and stared, blindly, at the screen. Fenella could see that there were tears in her eyes. She could guess what Mandy was about to write. Before she could stop herself, Fenella sat down at Ms Grimwood's desk and started to type.

Mandy heard the slight humming of Ms Grimwood's computer. She swivelled round in her chair and stared, open-mouthed, as the keys moved silently up and down and writing appeared on the screen.

> *I know what you're thinking, Mandy. I wish we could be proper friends as well.*

'Fen!' gasped Mandy. 'Are you really there? Sitting in Grimwood's chair?'

> *Yes,* typed Fenella. *I hope you're not scared.*

78

'No, of course not,' said Mandy. 'But why can't I *see* you again, like I did at Midwick Castle? Can't you materialise again – just for me? Then we could be proper friends.'

The old rules don't allow us to be friends with ordinary people. But they didn't say that we couldn't be COMPUTER friends.

Mandy laughed. 'No, I don't suppose they did. But what would happen if you broke the rules?'

I don't know. Nobody ever has.

'When I was at school,' said Mandy, 'I used to break the rules sometimes – the silly rules, not the sensible ones. This rule about not making friends with ordinary people sounds very silly to me.'

No writing appeared on Fenella's screen.

'Are you still there, Fen?' Mandy asked anxiously. 'I shouldn't have said anything about your rules. I'm sorry.'

That's okay, Fenella typed. *I agree with you. Give me time. I'm thinking.*

Fenella could think of no good reason for not having a proper friend. Perhaps no ghost had ever wanted one before. Anyway, she and her father were not like other ghosts. They didn't have to stick to the old rules. Some rules, silly rules, were just made to be broken.

If something *really* bad happened to those who broke the old rules – SHE WAS ABOUT TO FIND OUT…

'FEN!' Mandy stared at the girl, that strange yet familiar girl from the distant past, who was sitting rather stiffly in Ms Grimwood's chair.

Feeling oddly shy, Fenella stared back. With her flaming red hair, cheeks flushed with excitement, she did not look at all ghostlike.

'I can't believe it!' gasped Mandy. 'I can see you! Is it really you, Fen?'

'Who do you think it is?' demanded Fenella, beginning to enjoy herself. 'Old Grimwood? In disguise? Of course it's me, silly!'

The two girls giggled helplessly.

'Oh, Fen! I just can't believe that you're really here, talking to me!'

'We must keep it a secret,' warned Fenella. 'I know it's a stupid rule but Dad might…'

'MIGHT WHAT?' demanded a very angry voice from the back of the room.

The colour drained from Fenella's cheeks. She swivelled round in her chair.

There (seen and heard only by Fenella) stood her father. This time, not only was Fitzwizo not best pleased. He was *hopping mad*!

Eleven

Fenella had never known her father to be so angry. 'I trusted you, Fen! How *could* you sneak off and do something like this behind my back?'

'I didn't *sneak off*, Dad. I just came to check that Mandy had got my message.'

Mandy (who could see and hear only Fenella) was looking bewildered. 'What's going on, Fen? Who are you talking to?'

'It's my father,' Fenella explained. 'He's over there – at the back of the room. He's very angry with me.'

'And you can tell your friend – your *computer* friend,' said Fitzwizo, 'that I am not best pleased with her either. Did she put you up to this?'

'No, Dad, you can't blame Mandy. It was *my* decision. I decided to materialise.'

Mandy could guess what was going on. She looked towards the back of the room. 'I'm sorry. It was all my fault. I talked Fen into breaking the old rules.'

'No, you didn't!' protested Fenella.

'Yes, I did. And all I've done is get you into trouble. I'm sorry, Fen.' Mandy burst into tears. 'I only wanted to be friends,' she sobbed, 'proper friends.'

'Now look what you've done, Dad!' scolded Fen. 'You've upset Mandy.'

Fitzwizo sighed. This was more than he could cope with – *two* teenage girls on his hands! One was bad enough!

'Oh, all right,' he said gruffly. 'Tell your friend to stop snivelling. What's done is done. No good crying over spilt milk.'

'Dad says to stop crying, Mandy. He's not cross any more.'

'I jolly well am!' Fitzwizo protested indignantly. '*Very* cross! I just can't stand any more of that snivelling.'

Mandy wiped her eyes and blew her nose. She felt rather foolish as she addressed the bookcase at the back of the office. 'Thank you, Mr...er...er – what do I call your father, Fen?'

'His name is Sir Frederick Fitzwizo.'

'I'm very pleased to meet you, Sir Frederick.' Mandy frowned and turned to Fenella. 'Fitzwizo! That name rings a bell...I know – the Fitzwizos of Coldhill Castle! But...I saw you at Midwick Castle. I don't understand.'

Fitzwizo groaned. They couldn't possibly explain all that to Mandy – not now.

'I'll explain it all later,' Fenella said hastily, '*and* I'll tell you about Dingley Hall as well. Dad and I have to go now. We'll come back tomorrow and see what old

Grimwood has to say.'

'We're sure to lose our jobs,' Mandy said gloomily. 'I know you'd like to help, Fen, but I don't see how you can.'

'We can,' Fenella assured her. 'But you've *got* to come to Coldhill Castle with Ms Grimwood. When she sees all the ghostly activity that we've planned, she'll just *have* to believe you.'

Mandy's face brightened. 'The Coldhill Castle visit is down for Thursday. Ofspook couldn't possibly get a new team together before that. Your plan sounds great, Fen. I just hope it works.'

'Come on, Fen!' urged Fitzwizo. 'If they're coming on Thursday, we'll have to polish up our performance. Don't forget that our main aim is to get those starred phantoms – to save Coldhill Castle!'

'We've got to go and practise now, Mandy,' said Fen. 'See you soon. And try not to worry.'

'I'll try,' promised Mandy. 'And thanks for all your help – both of you. I feel a lot…'

Mandy's voice tailed away. Ms Grimwood's chair was empty. Her new friend, Fen, had vanished.

Mandy sighed. She was not looking forward to the next day, to Ms Grimwood's return. At least, whatever happened, she now knew that Fen would be around to help. She might not be able to save them but Mandy knew that her friend from the Middle Ages would do the very best she could.

When Fenella and Fitzwizo whirled down to the office

next day, they knew at once that the worst had happened.

'So,' Ms Grimwood was saying triumphantly, 'you are to clear your desks this afternoon. The new Ofspook team, chosen by the director and myself, will start work tomorrow.'

For once, Professor Pond was angry – very angry. 'This is most unfair, Ms Grimwood! We cannot be dismissed in this way. I would like to speak to the director myself – to put our case to him.'

'The director,' sneered Ms Grimwood, 'has no wish to speak to either of you. As your manager, I have told him all he needs to know. He has also read your reports. He cannot trust you to carry out any more investigations. That is why you must leave this afternoon.'

'Can't we just do one more visit – the one to Coldhill Castle?' asked Mandy.

'Certainly not! I can't imagine why you would even *want* to visit that boring old ruin.'

'She always calls it that!' fumed Fenella. 'I'd like to materialise right now and give that horrible woman a good fright. I *hate* her!'

'Calm down, Fen,' said her father. 'She won't find Coldhill Castle so boring when we've finished with her.'

'Mandy and the professor won't be able to come!' wailed Fenella. 'They're going to lose their jobs! We can't save them!'

'Our main aim,' Fitzwizo reminded her, 'is to get those starred phantoms – not to save your friends.'

'I know that, Dad. But we could have done *both*. We

84

could have got our phantoms *and* saved their jobs at the same time.'

Fitzwizo was looking thoughtful. 'Perhaps we still can, Fen. I've just thought of a plan.'

At lunchtime, when the office was empty, Fitzwizo sat down at Ms Grimwood's computer. 'Stand by the door, Fen,' he ordered, 'and tell me if anyone's coming.'

Quickly, he started to type:

> *TO*
> *Miss Grimwood*
> *Following our meeting yesterday, I have had another look at the Ofspook rules. I find that Professor Pond and Ms Day cannot be dismissed immediately. The regulations permit them to stay until the end of the week. I'm afraid that they will have to accompany you to Coldhill Castle, the next site on your list. I am sorry about this.*
> *Please inform the new members of the Ofspook team that they will not begin work until next Monday. You will be unable to contact me during the rest of this week as I am going abroad on business.*
> *FROM*
> *George Grey*
> *Director, Ofspook.*

'Dad!' Fenella, standing behind his chair, was impressed. 'That's brilliant! Do you think she'll fall for it?'

'I hope so. But *you're* supposed to be keeping watch, Fen.'

Fenella scampered back to the door – just in time. 'Quick, Dad! They're coming!' Hastily, Fitzwizo cleared the computer screen, leaving only the small green envelope.

Ms Grimwood's mouth tightened as she read the message from the director. She turned to Mandy and the professor.

'It seems that, under your contract, Ofspook has to employ you for the rest of the week. As you know, I had hoped that my new, efficient team would start work tomorrow. Instead, I shall have to put up with you two for a few more days.'

'Does that mean that we'll be going to Coldhill Castle?' asked Mandy.

'Yes, I'm afraid it does. Fortunately, that will be your last assignment.'

'Well done, Dad!' cried Fenella, hugging her father. 'You're a genius!'

'I wouldn't go as far as that,' Fitzwizo protested modestly. 'Above average, perhaps. But now we must get back to base, Fen. We have some final preparations to make.'

Twelve

All was quiet at Coldhill Castle when the Ofspook team arrived. 'As I thought,' sniffed Ms Grimwood, looking around scornfully, 'we might as well not bother with this place.'

'You never know,' said Mandy, smiling. 'You might be in for a surprise.'

'I doubt it, Ms Day. I doubt it very much – unless your over-active imagination comes up with something, as it usually does.'

'Mandy does not imagine…' Professor Pond began indignantly, but Ms Grimwood had marched off to look at the view.

'Don't worry, Professor,' said Mandy. 'Everything will be all right. You'll see.'

Professor Pond was puzzled. 'I don't understand. Why are you in such good spirits today?'

'Good spirits!' giggled Mandy. 'I like that!'

'It wasn't meant to be a joke. Have you forgotten that

we are about to lose our jobs?' He peered at her suspiciously. 'Do you know something that I don't?'

Mandy stopped laughing. 'Yes, I do. We won't lose our jobs, Professor, because...' She dropped her voice as Ms Grimwood came striding towards them. 'I'll tell you all about it – later.'

'Well,' said Ms Grimwood, 'I can't say I'm looking forward to spending the night in this ghastly place.'

'*Ghostly*? Did you say *ghostly*?' asked Mandy. 'Have you seen something strange?'

'No, I have not – and I said *ghastly*, not *ghostly*, as you very well know. I'm surprised that you feel like making one of your little jokes, Ms Day. Have you forgotten that this is your very last assignment?'

'No,' said Mandy cheerfully. 'I haven't forgotten. But we've got to keep our spirits up – don't you think so, Ms Grimwood?'

'Now,' interrupted Professor Pond, before Ms Grimwood could answer, 'we must get down to work. I want to do some measuring before the light fades.'

Mandy and the professor took photographs, recorded measurements and studied a plan of Coldhill Castle as it used to be.

'Our boss isn't much help,' said Mandy. 'She's just gone back to the car.'

'Well, she's not sitting in the car all night,' said the professor crossly. 'The director has asked her to watch us. We'll make sure that she does – whether she likes it or not.'

It was not often that Professor Pond sounded so fierce.

'You don't much like Ms Grimwood, do you?' asked Mandy.

'No, I do not.' The professor sighed wistfully. 'I just wish that this place could turn out like Dingley Hall and Midwick Castle – with lots of ghostly activity. That would show... *what was that*?'

In the fading light, a blood-curdling scream (one of Lady Marigold's best) echoed around the castle walls.

'I have a feeling, Professor Pond,' said Mandy, smiling, 'that your wish is about to come true.'

'Was that all right, dear?' Lady Marigold asked anxiously. 'I was a bit nervous, you know. It's hundreds of years since I've done my scream for an audience.'

'Very good, Marigold,' Fitzwizo reassured her. 'Just the sort of scream I was looking for.'

Fitzwizo's plan was that *Operation Phantom* would concentrate first on Category A in the Ofspook guidelines – *GHOSTLY SOUNDS*.

'Well done, Mum!' said Fenella. 'Even Ms Grimwood can't explain *that* away.'

But Ms Grimwood could. She had left the car and joined Mandy and the professor.

'I expect,' she sneered, 'that you two, left to yourselves, would call that noise a ghostly scream.'

'Both ghostly and ghastly, I'd say,' giggled Mandy.

Ms Grimwood gave her an icy stare. 'It is just as well

that I am here to supervise you, Ms Day. As you know, this castle stands on a high hill, exposed to the elements. That noise was merely the wind whistling around the castle walls – nothing more.'

They did not know that Fenella was standing beside them, listening carefully. 'Wind indeed!' she muttered crossly. 'We'll soon put the wind up *you*, Ms Grimwood!'

She reported back to her father.

'Right!' said Fitzwizo. 'I think another of your special screams is called for, Marigold.'

'Oh, dear!' flapped Lady Marigold. 'Are you sure, Frederick? I . . . I think I've got stage fright. I don't think I can do it again.'

'Mother!' said Percival sternly. 'This is for the honour of the Fitzwizos. It is your *duty* to scream again.'

'Yes, dear, I suppose you're right.' Lady Marigold cleared her throat. 'Well – here goes!' She gathered her breath.

The scream that followed was, without a doubt, the most ghostly, most ghastly, most blood-curdling scream that Lady Marigold had ever produced. As it echoed and re-echoed around the castle walls, even Fenella felt slightly shivery.

'Wow, Mum! That was some sound! That was *really* spooky!'

'I was rather pleased with that one myself,' said Lady Marigold. 'I've got over my stage fright now, Frederick. Would you like me to do another one?'

'No, thank you, dear,' Fitzwizo said hastily, as his

wife opened her mouth wide in readiness, 'that should be enough to do the trick.'

Mandy thought so too. Even in the dusk she could see that Ms Grimwood had gone very pale and was looking around nervously.

'Extraordinary!' exclaimed Professor Pond. 'I'm glad my sound recorder was switched on. As you were saying, Ms Grimwood, the wind does create some very strange sound effects at this height – very strange indeed.'

'I'm glad you explained all that about the wind,' said Mandy. 'Otherwise, you know me, I might have imagined it was a ghost.'

For once, Ms Grimwood had nothing to say. She sank down heavily on to one of their picnic chairs and, rather shakily, poured herself a mug of strong coffee.

'That flask of coffee has to last all night,' protested Mandy, before she could stop herself. 'You can't drink it *now*!'

Ms Grimwood was beginning to recover. 'If you don't mind, Ms Day, that is for *me* to decide. I am in charge of this investigation.'

By this time it was dark, with a full moon – just the sort of night that Fitzwizo had hoped for. It was time for Percival (unseen but *heard*) to clank about in his suit of armour. He had assured his father that he would not fall over this time.

CLANK! CLANK! CLANK!

'Goodness!' Professor Pond switched on his sound

recorder. 'Do you think it's that noisy old wind again, Ms Grimwood?'

The sound was getting louder – and *closer*.

CLANK! CLANK! CLANK!

Then————————**CRAAAASH**!

'Wh-what was that?' Ms Grimwood jumped to her feet, spilling her mug of coffee. 'What was that noise?'

'You tell us,' said the professor. 'You're the expert.'

'You're not frightened, are you, Ms Grimwood?' asked Mandy.

'Of course not! There's bound to be a logical explanation. There always is.'

'Left to myself,' said Mandy, 'I might have said that it sounded very much like a medieval knight clomping around in full armour. But then, I expect that's just my over-active imagination.'

'And that almighty crash sounded as if he'd just tripped over something,' said the professor. 'You've got it, Mandy! A very noisy knight!'

'Not a silent knight, that's for sure,' giggled Mandy. 'Get it? Silent night – silent kn…'

'Stop this nonsense at once!' barked Ms Grimwood. 'You should be looking for an explanation, Ms Day, not making one of your silly jokes.'

With that, she sat down again and poured herself a fresh mug of coffee.

'Mandy,' said Professor Pond, picking up his torch, 'could you come and help me for a moment? I want to check something over by the East Tower.'

'You don't mind being left alone for a little while, do you, Ms Grimwood?' asked Mandy. 'You won't be frightened?'

'Me?' snorted Ms Grimwood. 'Frightened? Don't be ridiculous, Ms Day.'

'I just wanted to get away from her for a few minutes,' said Professor Pond, shining his torch on the crumbling walls of the East Tower. 'I think you should tell me what's going on.'

'You're not going to find this easy to believe,' warned Mandy.

She was right.

'Incredible!' As he listened, Professor Pond shook his head in amazement. 'Simply incredible!'

'But you do believe me?' Mandy asked anxiously as they walked back towards Ms Grimwood.

'Of course I do. This is all very exciting, Mandy. We must make full use of sound recorders and cameras – and just hope that they work this time. I wonder what will happen next!'

Fitzwizo, as you can imagine, was not best pleased with Percival's clumsy performance. But, as Fenella pointed out, that final crash had certainly put the wind up Ms Grimwood.

What with all the fuss in helping Percy to his feet, Fenella was a bit late with her own sound effect.

She had decided to specialise in strange, horrible

laughs. She'd got the idea from a film on TV called *House of Hideous Laughter*. In the film, the people who lived in this house were always terrified by strange, ghostly, unexplained laughter. Needless to say, they soon sold up and moved.

'Wait a minute, Fen,' directed Fitzwizo. 'We've got to get the timing right.'

After that second mug of coffee, Ms Grimwood was back to her old self. She stood up as Mandy and the professor approached. 'Well, team,' she announced briskly, 'I have been thinking about all those strange sounds. There is absolutely nothing for you to be frightened of.'

'*We* weren't frightened,' murmured Mandy.

Ms Grimwood ignored her. 'As I thought, there is a perfectly logical explanation.'

'What a relief!' exclaimed Professor Pond. 'So you don't think it has anything at all to do with ghosts then?'

'Certainly not! Let me explain, Professor. The few visitors who come here probably leave cans and other rubbish behind. When tin cans and suchlike are blown about by the wind, it could sound like...'

Her jaw dropped as peal after peal of strange, terrifying, ghostly laughter echoed and re-echoed around the moonlit castle walls. This was real *House of Hideous Laughter* stuff – Fenella's best.

'Wow!' gasped Mandy. 'How many tin cans would it take to make that noise, Ms Grimwood?'

There was no reply.

As the weird sounds began to fade, Fenella raced from the East Tower to the West Tower and started again. She was enjoying herself now – really getting into the spirit of the thing!

The dreadful, ghostly, ghastly laughter seemed to bounce and echo from every side. To round off the performance, Fenella threw in a few monstrous moans and hideous howls. It was all more than enough to make you move house – or move castle!

'I'm sure that was Fen,' Mandy whispered to the professor.

'So *that* was your friend. I'm impressed. A very *spirited* performance!'

Mandy giggled. It was not often that Professor Pond made a little joke.

Ms Grimwood was not laughing. She was standing bolt upright, listening intently. 'What was that? That strange scraping noise?'

Fitzwizo was feeling a bit of a twit as he dragged a huge bunch of rusty old chains across the stone floor. On TV, ghosts often seemed to clank about in heavy chains. It made a very satisfactory noise and, for some reason, always seemed to terrify people.

'To me, that sounds like heavy chains being dragged across the floor,' said Mandy. 'And I'm almost sure I can hear footsteps. But then – that's little old me! You know what my imagination is like.'

'Whatever it is, I'm recording it,' said the professor.

'What do you think it is this time, Ms Grimwood?'

Ms Grimwood did not reply. She was standing with her back pressed tight against the castle wall, looking around fearfully.

'It's getting louder!' she said in a hoarse whisper. 'It's getting closer!'

By this time Fitzwizo had had enough. The chains were very heavy and, as Lady Marigold kept reminding him, he wasn't getting any younger. Also, he didn't want to frighten Ms Grimwood any more at this stage. That was not part of the plan.

He abandoned the chains and called a meeting in the East Tower.

'Well done, team!' he said in his best Police Inspector tone. '*Operation Phantom* is on target. So far – so good.'

'Old Grimwood was really rattled by those chains, Dad,' said Fenella.

Fitzwizo smiled modestly. 'Yes, I think that sound did have the desired effect. Now we'll see what she makes of Category B – *GHOSTLY SIGHTINGS*. The best is yet to come!'

Thirteen

'Now don't forget,' warned Fitzwizo. 'This time we are concentrating on Category B – *GHOSTLY SIGHTINGS*. We are to be *SEEN* but not *HEARD*.'

Lady Marigold was not at all nervous about this bit. After all these centuries, floating through walls was second nature to her. Unfortunately, she chose to make her entrance right next to where Ms Grimwood was standing with her back pressed against the wall. They did not see each other.

But, as the moon came out from behind a cloud, Professor Pond and Mandy could see both of them – very clearly. They stared in amazement as Lady Marigold began, slowly and gracefully, to make her entrance.

'I'm sure that's Lady Marigold Fitzwizo,' whispered Mandy. 'I've read all about her.'

Quickly, the professor seized his camera. 'Could you move a little to the left, Ms Grimwood?' he asked, looking through the view-finder. 'Then I can get both of you in.'

'*Both* of us? What *are* you talking about?' demanded Ms Grimwood. 'And why are you taking a photograph of me?'

'Not only you,' said the professor. 'You and the lady beside you.'

'Don't be ridiculous!' Ms Grimwood stared fiercely around. 'There's no...'

Her mouth dropped open as she came face to face with Lady Marigold, whose head was now free of the wall.

Lady Marigold froze – petrified by Ms Grimwood's fierce stare. Close up, this woman was even more terrifying than she had imagined! Hastily, Lady Marigold tried to go into reverse. She couldn't. Still frozen with fear, she could move neither backwards nor forwards.

For the first time in her afterlife, Lady Marigold was firmly stuck in the thick castle wall. She could move only those parts of her body that were free of the stone. Frantically, she wiggled her head, her forearms, her ankles and feet.

Ms Grimwood stared in horror as Lady Marigold struggled to get free. Then, with a soft moan, she fell to the ground.

Lady Marigold looked down in surprise. Ms Grimwood, slumped at her feet, no longer had the power to terrify her. She began to relax. Once more, she felt light and ready to float.

'Could you hold it there, please, Your Ladyship?' asked Professor Pond. 'I'd like to take some more photographs.'

Obligingly, almost out of the wall, Lady Marigold paused. Carefully, she rearranged the folds of her silken gown and pulled her golden tresses free of the stone. Knowing that she was looking her very best, she smiled sweetly for the camera.

Then, slowly, dreamily, she floated free of the wall – and vanished into thin air.

'Oh, dear!' said Mandy. 'We've forgotten all about Ms Grimwood. I think she's coming round.'

Ms Grimwood was now sitting up, holding her head in her hands, groaning loudly.

'Are you feeling better now?' asked Professor Pond, helping her to her chair.

'I'm not surprised that you fainted,' said Mandy, getting out the thermos flask. 'You've had a bad shock. I think we should all have some strong black coffee – *if* there's any left. This castle is getting *really* exciting!'

'Exciting!' muttered Ms Grimwood, gulping her coffee. 'Is that what you call it?'

'Oh, yes,' said the professor. '*Very* exciting. This level of ghostly activity is quite incredible.'

'Even *you* can't deny it this time, Ms Grimwood,' said Mandy. 'You saw Lady Marigold, didn't you? That's why you fainted.'

Ms Grimwood was beginning to recover. 'I *thought* I saw something,' she admitted. 'Of course it could have been the moon shining on stone – a trick of the light.'

'That was no trick of the light,' said Mandy firmly. 'That was Lady Marigold Fitzwizo, floating right through the castle wall. Only a ghost could...'

'Look!' Professor Pond interrupted. 'Over there! By the West Tower!'

This was Percival's big moment. He stood tall (as tall as he could) and proud. He looked every inch (or should I say *every centimetre*?) a knight. Slowly, carefully, he began to pace towards the Ofspook team.

'What did I tell you?' giggled Mandy. 'Here comes our silent knight!'

'He's coming closer!' gasped Ms Grimwood, shrinking back into her chair. 'Do something, Professor!'

'I am doing something. I'm taking photographs.'

'I'd like a photo of him for myself,' said Mandy. 'I think he's cute.'

Percival heard that. *Cute*! His sister used that word sometimes. He did not like it. He, a Fitzwizo of Coldhill Castle, might be described as *noble, dignified, distinguished* – certainly not *cute!*

He felt so cross that he de-materialised on the spot. These people did not deserve to look upon him.

'He heard that,' said Professor Pond. 'He didn't like it.'

'Oh dear!' said Mandy, guessing that Percival was still within earshot. 'I didn't mean to offend him. When I say *cute*, I mean *really impressive*. And I bet, under that helmet, he's ever so handsome as well.'

Mandy was right. Percival was within earshot. He

forgave Mandy at once. She was obviously a very intelligent girl. He decided to make one more appearance, at the top of the East Tower.

'There he is again!' cried the professor, pointing.

The East Tower was not, now, as tall as it once had been. Nevertheless, at that height, spotlit by the moon, Percival *did* look impressive. As they stared up at him, he removed his helmet and tucked it under his arm. He hoped that, even at this distance, Mandy could see that she was right. He *was* a rather handsome knight.

'Stop posing!' hissed Fenella, who had scampered up what remained of the spiral staircase. 'Dad says you've got to stop now. You're way over your time.'

Before he de-materialised, Percival gave the Ofspook team a royal wave. 'By the way,' he said, as he followed Fenella down the stairs, 'your friend Mandy seems to think that I'm rather... er... handsome.'

'Does she now?' chuckled Fenella. 'You should carry your head under your arm, Percy, like some ghosts. Then you'd look *really* handsome.'

'Very funny!' sneered Percival. 'You're on next. Let's see how well *you* do.'

To tell the truth, Fenella was not altogether happy about her part in *Operation Phantom*. The hideous laughter bit had been okay but as for making a personal appearance...

'Over there!' Mandy exclaimed excitedly, pointing towards the entrance to the East Tower. 'Looks to me like another medieval lady, Ms Grimwood.' She turned to the professor and whispered proudly, 'It's Fen. That's my friend, Fen!'

In her tall hat, carrying her candle, Fenella looked as if she were sleep-walking. Head held high, she walked slowly, very slowly, towards the Ofspook team.

'Another trick of the light – eh, Ms Grimwood?' asked Professor Pond, as he started on a new roll of film.

'She's coming towards us!' gasped Ms Grimwood. 'What is it? Who is she?'

Fenella stood still, a few paces away from them, candleholder at arm's length. Luckily, her hat had not fallen off – not even once. That would have spoilt the effect.

'Go away!' Ms Grimwood shouted suddenly. She jumped to her feet, knocking her chair to the ground. She faced Fenella. 'Whoever you are – GO AWAY!'

Professor Pond switched on his sound recorder. 'You believe in ghosts now – don't you, Ms Grimwood?'

Ms Grimwood stared at the professor. She stared at the tape recorder.

'I know what you're up to,' she hissed. 'You're trying to trap me. You want me to say that I've seen ghosts here. You want it on tape.'

'Yes,' said the professor quietly, 'I want you to tell the truth.'

'Well, I *won't* say it!' snarled Ms Grimwood. 'Knowing you two, this could all be a trick.'

'A trick, Ms Grimwood?' asked Mandy.

'Yes, Ms Day. One of your silly jokes. I heard you whispering something about a friend.' She stared at Fenella and laughed wildly. 'That's it! This girl is a friend of yours, dressed up to look like a ghost. Well, you can't fool me, you know!'

'So,' Mandy said quietly, 'you don't think that this could possibly be the ghost of Fenella Fitzwizo, of Coldhill Castle?'

'Of course I don't! You and the professor planned all this to try to save your jobs. Well – you won't get away with it. I'll see to that!'

Fenella sighed. There was only one thing for it now! She did *not* want to do this. She did *not*. It was not part of the plan. But, for Mandy's sake, it had to be done. Slowly, very slowly, she walked towards Ms Grimwood.

Defiantly, Ms Grimwood stood her ground. Candle in hand, eyes closed, Fenella kept on going.

'Go aw…aaaagh!' Ms Grimwood staggered, choking in disbelief and horror as Fenella walked straight through her. A sharp burning feeling (from the candle) was followed by a cold, clammy, shivery sensation – unlike anything that she had ever experienced before. She stumbled to the nearest chair and sat down heavily.

Fenella wasn't feeling much better. For one awful moment she had been afraid that she might get stuck, inside Ms Grimwood, like her mother in the wall. A wall was one thing, but Ms Grimwood – ugh! It didn't bear thinking about.

Well, she'd done her bit – beyond the call of duty –

for Mandy and for Coldhill Castle. It was her father's turn now. If all went according to plan, this part of the performance should also take care of Category C in the Ofspook guidelines – *GHOSTLY ATMOSPHERE*.

Mandy and the professor stared in amazement as Sir Frederick Fitzwizo, cloak wrapped around him, came whirling over the castle wall. He did a few extra spins in mid-air and landed neatly beside what remained of the medieval fireplace. Ms Grimwood, still dazed from her last experience, did not even look surprised.

Facing the fireplace, Fitzwizo waved his arms about a bit. Although he was chanting the words of an old Fitzwizo wizard's spell, the Ofspook team could hear nothing.

'I wonder what he's up to,' said the professor.

'I don't know,' said Mandy. 'But I have feeling that something very strange is about to happen.'

She was right. As Fitzwizo stepped back, the medieval fireplace burst into life. Flames roared up from huge logs – logs which had not been there a moment ago. As Mandy and the professor stared at the fire, they had a feeling that everything around them was shifting and changing.

'We're in the Great Hall!' gasped the professor. 'As it used to be! I don't believe it!'

But it was true. It had all, through the old Fitzwizo magic, been restored and recreated. There was a fresh covering of reeds under their feet and a beamed roof, instead of the sky, above their heads. Colourful banners hung from the walls.

Before they had time to take in any more details, Fitzwizo raised his hand.

Suddenly – there was sound. It was the sound of an unseen minstrel playing on a lute – a sound, soft and beautiful, that none of them had ever heard before.

As if conjured up by the medieval music, Lady Marigold, Fenella and Percival made their entrance. Percival, in a yellow fur-trimmed tunic and matching cloak, was (in his own opinion at least) looking very handsome indeed. Slowly, they made their way to the high table at the far end of the room. This table, now magically laden with food and drink, was raised above the level of the rest of the hall.

As Fitzwizo joined his family, the minstrel music changed to a lively happy tune – a tune that Sir Frederick and Lady Marigold had often danced to in the olden days. All the old Fitzwizo magic was in the air as the unseen minstrel played – louder and louder, faster and faster.

Suddenly, the Great Hall, with its bright banners and dancing flames, spun dizzily around the Ofspook team – and vanished.

They were back in the present – no blazing fire, no feast, no minstrel song. Instead, as if nothing whatsoever had happened, the moon shone coldly on the ruined castle walls. The wind had dropped. The night was very still.

'Phew!' said Mandy, breaking the silence at last. 'That was quite a show! You saw it too, Ms Grimwood. You can't deny it this time.'

But, even now, Ms Grimwood could! She sprang to her feet and glared defiantly at Mandy and the professor.

'I don't care what I saw or heard! I shall deny everything. It's your word against mine. On your past record, who do you think is going to believe you two?'

'I AM – FOR ONE!'

They spun round as a tall, fair-haired man stepped out of the shadows behind them and into the moonlight.

This time, Ms Grimwood *did* look as if she'd just seen a ghost. For the fair-haired man was Mr Grey – director of Ofspook!

Fourteen

'Mr Gr-Gr-Grey!' stammered Ms Grimwood. 'I thought you were abr-abr-abroad.'

'Abroad, Ms Grimwood? Whatever gave you that idea?'

'Your m-message. You said…'

'I don't know what you're talking about,' Mr Grey interrupted coldly. 'When I contacted your office today I was told that you had come up here. Are these the two people mentioned in your reports – Professor Pond and Ms Day?'

'Y-y-yes,' babbled Ms Grimwood. 'But…I-I've changed my mind about them, Mr Grey. I really have. I was just going to tell you how…'

'**YOU**,' thundered Mr Grey, 'were going to tell me that these two good people were lying – that none of these amazing things ever happened. Fortunately, I decided to do some investigating on my own. I parked my car a little way down the hill so that you would not hear me approach. *You* are the liar, Ms Grimwood. I saw and heard everything.'

He turned to Mandy and the professor. 'I owe you two an apology. I was not entirely happy with Ms Grimwood's reports. When I heard that you were still working for Ofspook, I decided to follow you here. That has told me all I need to know.'

'So we won't lose our jobs?' asked Mandy.

'Certainly not! I'm most impressed with your work.' Mr Grey looked at his watch. 'Two a.m. Since you've been up all night, take the rest of the morning off. We'll have an Ofspook meeting in your office at three o'clock this afternoon.'

'We told the truth in all our reports, Mr Grey,' said Professor Pond.

'I know that now. And if I hadn't seen all this incredible ghostly activity with my own eyes, I would not have believed you this time. I would have believed your head of department. I have had bad reports about her behaviour in other offices. I should have checked up on her before this. Because of this woman's lies, you might both have lost your jobs.'

'That's not true!' Ms Grimwood protested wildly. 'I-I was going to...'

'I *know* what you were going to do,' snapped Mr Grey. 'You can't lie to me any more, Ms Grimwood. I shall now give you a lift home in my car. There are some matters that I would like to discuss – in private.'

*

'Well, Mandy,' said Professor Pond, 'I think we can be satisfied with our night's work.'

'Thanks to the Fitzwizos of Coldhill Castle! I wish I could see Fen before we go. I just hope she's okay – especially after walking right through old Grimwood.'

'She's a brave girl,' said the professor. 'It must have been an awful experience.'

'You can say that again!' Fenella, minus tall hat and candle, suddenly appeared beside them. 'That was the most horrible experience of my afterlife – a lot more ghastly than ghostly.'

'Must have taken real guts to do that, Fen,' giggled Mandy.

'Ha! Ha! Very funny. It was no joke, I can tell you.'

'I'm sure it wasn't,' said Professor Pond. 'Aren't you going to introduce me to this young lady, Mandy?'

'Meet Fenella Fitzwizo, Professor Pond,' Mandy said proudly. 'This is my friend – Fen.'

'I'm very pleased to meet you, Fenella,' said the professor, 'and very grateful to you and your family. Would it be possible to thank them properly – in person, as it were?'

'No, I'm afraid not. You see, they don't believe in talking to people – people who aren't ghosts, that is. It's against the old rules.'

'Was your mum mad at you for being my friend?' asked Mandy.

'She was at first. She's even a bit nervous about me talking to you now. But Dad told her that it's useful to have a go-between, to pass messages between ghosts and people.'

'Especially one that can use the computer,' laughed Professor Pond.

'Yes,' agreed Fenella, 'that did help.'

'Talking of computers,' said Mandy, 'I think you and your father should be at the Ofspook meeting this afternoon.'

'We'll be there,' promised Fenella. 'It could be important.'

The meeting that afternoon was *very* important – for all of them. Apart from their head of department, they were all there on time. Fitzwizo and Fenella (once more unseen and unheard) waited impatiently for the meeting to begin.

'Ms Grimwood will not be attending this meeting,' announced Mr Grey. 'She will not be returning to the office. Ms Grimwood has been dismissed. After all her lies, it is *she* who has lost her job – not you.'

'I can't say I'm sorry,' said Professor Pond. 'Does that mean we'll have a new head of department?'

'That is the first item on our agenda,' said Mr Grey. 'I take it that you do not want any extra responsibility, Professor Pond?'

'No,' said the professor. 'That's why I retired from my job at the university.'

'In that case,' said Mr Grey, 'I would like to offer the post of head of department to Ms Day.'

'To me?' Mandy was astonished.

'Why not?' demanded Professor Pond. 'You would make an excellent manager, Mandy.'

'I agree,' said Mr Grey. 'I know that you are very young, Ms Day, but I have been most impressed with your work. I also know that I can trust you. You would immediately take over Ms Grimwood's responsibilities and salary. Will you accept this post?'

Mandy still looked dazed. 'Well...er...yes, thank you, Mr Grey.'

'Good. That's that, then. Now – do you need another assistant? It would be helpful if you could manage without. Ofspook is rather short of funds at the moment.'

'I'm sure that we can manage on our own,' said Mandy.

Professor Pond agreed. 'Of course we can. Mandy and I always did most of the work anyway.'

'And I have a friend,' said Mandy, 'who might be willing to help out from time to time – at no extra cost. She's already been in a few times to do a bit of work for us. She likes to practise her computer skills.'

'Excellent!' said Mr Grey. 'I'm surprised that Ms Grimwood never mentioned her.'

'She's a very quiet worker,' said Professor Pond. 'I expect Ms Grimwood hardly noticed she was there.'

Mr Grey laughed. 'Sounds as if your friend is almost invisible, Ms Day. You could call her your *ghost writer* – very suitable for Ofspook!'

'*Ghost writer,*' repeated Mandy, smiling. 'That's a good name for her. She'd like that.'

Fenella, who was listening carefully, *did* like it. She clutched her father's arm. 'That's me, Dad! They mean me! I'm going to be Mandy's assistant – on the computer!'

'Sssh!' Fitzwizo put his finger to his lips. 'Listen!'

'Next item,' Mr Grey was saying, 'Coldhill Castle.'

'We haven't had time to do our report yet,' said Mandy.

'I don't need to see your report, Ms Day. I was there – remember? If I could award that place *fifty* starred phantoms, I would. As it is, Coldhill Castle will have the maximum allowed – FIVE STARRED PHANTOMS!'

Fitzwizo hugged his daughter excitedly. 'We've done it, Fen! We've got our five starred phantoms!'

'I can't believe it!' gasped Fenella. 'It's all thanks to you, Dad – to *Operation Phantom*. Just wait until we tell…'

'Sssh!'

'You mean,' said Mandy, 'that Coldhill Castle might get some money from the National Lottery?'

'I very much hope so,' said Mr Grey. 'When *the Good Ghost Guide* is published, Coldhill Castle will attract a lot of visitors. I shall put in a bid for a substantial amount of money – enough to rebuild much of the castle, to restore it to its former glory.'

'Our *ghost writer* will be pleased to hear that,' said Professor Pond.

'Does she have a special interest in Coldhill Castle?' asked Mr Grey.

'Oh, yes,' said Mandy. 'My friend is very attached to the place.'

'Well, that's that, then,' said Mr Grey, gathering up his papers. 'Now, I would like to invite both of you to join me for dinner – to celebrate Ms Day's promotion and the newly discovered wonders of Coldhill Castle. What a pity your friend isn't here as well, Ms Day.'

'Yes,' said Mandy. 'She'd love to celebrate. We could say that she's with us in spirit.'

'Speaking of which,' laughed Mr Grey, looking around the office, 'I can see why we never come across any haunted office blocks. An ancient castle is one thing but can you imagine any self-respecting ghost taking a fancy to this place.'

'Oh, I don't know,' said Mandy. 'There's no accounting for taste!'

'This is our lucky day!' chortled Fitzwizo, when the others had left the room. 'Lots of visitors! Coldhill Castle restored! Come on, Fen! I can't wait to tell your mother and Percy about all this.'

'Wait a sec, Dad! I want to leave a message for Mandy.'

Next morning, Mandy was not at all surprised to see the little green envelope on her computer screen. As she thought, the message was from Fen.

Dear Mandy,
Congratulations! You'll be a brilliant
manager. Just don't become like old
Grimwood – only joking! By the way, I'm
very happy to accept the job of office
assistant (ghost writer!). What with that
and acting as a 'go-between', my afterlife
is going to be pretty busy from now on.
Dad and I are thrilled about our five
starred phantoms! We're off to give Mum
and Percy the good news.
See you soon,
From
YOUR BEST FRIEND EVER,
Fen

Fifteen

And there we will have to leave Mandy and the professor and the Fitzwizos of Coldhill Castle.

But I can tell you that they *did* get the highest rating in the *Good Ghost Guide* and they *did* get a large sum of money from the National Lottery – enough, as Mr Grey had hoped, to restore much of the castle to its former glory. Nowadays, visitors come from far and wide. You yourself – who knows? – may one day find yourself at this ancient castle.

Lady Marigold, as she drifts around her ancestral home, is delighted by all the changes. When she chooses to make a personal appearance, there are many more walls for her to float through. With her long golden tresses and her beautiful gowns, she is much admired by the tourists. She is happier than she has been for hundreds of years.

So is Percival. He keeps his armour polished and ready at all times. He does not, of course, make a public appearance unless he approves of the visitors. Some of them, in his opinion, are altogether too noisy and common to look upon a Fitzwizo of Coldhill Castle. So, if you do go there, make sure that you are on your best behaviour!

When Percival does appear, pacing the length of the newly-restored battlements, the tourists are always suitably impressed. As you can imagine, he is a great favourite with the young ladies – their knight in shining armour!

The tourists see much less of Sir Frederick Fitzwizo and his daughter, Fenella. To please her mother, Fenella materialises at Coldhill Castle from time to time. But, to be honest, she finds that part of her afterlife pretty boring. She is much more interested in her job as office assistant. She is no longer just a noble young lady from the Middle Ages. She has a job. Like her friend Mandy, she is a busy working girl.

Fitzwizo himself is very proud of their five starred phantoms. Now and again, to keep up the ghostly atmosphere, he clanks about a bit with his rusty chains. He is also very proud of his restored ancestral home. But it is still a medieval castle – and he still prefers the new town at the foot of the hill. He can travel up and down in comfort now, as the visitors come and go in their buses and cars.

Just to keep him on his toes (or rather, *off* his toes) Fenella insists that they still, sometimes, use the old whirling technique. After all, they have the wizardly blood of those distant ancestors in their veins. They do not want to lose any of that magic power.

For without that ancient power they would not have known about Ofspook or the *Good Ghost Guide*. Mandy and Fenella would never have met. Coldhill Castle would not have been saved.

Fenella and her father know how important that ancient power has been. They – and even you, if you visit Coldhill Castle! – have every reason to be grateful to those old Fitzwizo wizards.

Other Paperback Fiction Titles from
Andersen Press

TIGER Series

THE WITCH-BABY
Cara Lockhart Smith
Illustrated by Bridget MacKeith

When Sophie Starling agrees to look after an abandoned Witch-Baby for the day, she soon finds she has taken on more than she bargained for. 'A funny and often irreverent story for emerging readers, greatly enhanced by lively and amusing illustrations.'
School Librarian

0 86264 800 9   80pp   ages 6 - 9

ANDERSEN YOUNG READERS' LIBRARY

GRISEL AND THE TOOTH FAIRY and Other Stories
Roger Collinson
Illustrated by Tony Ross

A hilarious collection of short stories about the wayward and spirited Griselda, otherwise known as Grisel. This is a companion volume to Roger Collinson's comic *Willy* stories - 'Willy is a modern "Just William".' - *School Librarian*

0 86264 689 8   80pp

O'DRISCOLL'S TREASURE
Patrick Cooper

An exciting story set in Western Ireland by a new author to the Andersen list. A group of children set out to foil development plans for their island home and to find the previous owner's 'treasure'.

0 86264 839 4   96pp

THE GHOST OF TANTONY PIG
Julia Jarman
Illustrated by Laszlo Acs

'A spooksome read of a talking porker with a mysterious secret.
You'll be gripped.' *Young Telegraph*

0 86264 795 9   144pp

WHEN POPPY RAN AWAY
Julia Jarman
Illustrated by Karen Elliott

Poppy Field isn't sure what she *meant* to do to prissy Virginia
Creeber, when they were playing together, but she is sure she
shouldn't be around when the grown-ups discover what she *has*
done. 'Characters, both child and adult, are credible and
convincing.' *British Book News*

0 86264 794 0   128pp

BOY MISSING!
Hazel Townson
Illustrated by Tony Ross

Jeremy is surprised not to be met at the station on his return from
boarding school for the holidays. When a girl turns up saying
that the family car has broken down outside her house, he decides
to follow her - only to find he has walked into a trap.

0 86264 889 0   80pp

DISASTER BAG
Hazel Townson
Illustrated by David McKee

Colin Laird thinks he has protected himself against all
eventualities with his Disaster Bag, but he has reckoned without
terrorist Ruby Rugg. 'One of Townson's best.' - *Books for Keeps*

0 86264 524 7   80pp

RUMPUS ON THE ROOF
Hazel Townson
Illustrated by David McKee

Undersized Harry proves himself a hero when his next door
neighbour is threatened by villains. 'Racy, entertaining storylines
typify Townson.' - *Books for Keeps*

0 86264 591 3   80pp

TROUBLE DOUBLED
Hazel Townson

Two exciting mysteries - *Dads at the Double* and *Double Snatch* -
both revealed through letters, are combined in this paperback
original. 'The action is artfully advanced through
correspondence.' - *Daily Telegraph*

0 86264 710 X   144pp

TROUBLE ON THE TRAIN
A Lenny & Jake Adventure
Hazel Townson
Illustrated by Philippe Dupasquier

On a train trip to a Manchester museum, Lenny overhears a
sinister-sounding conversation. He tries to pass on a warning but
nobody will believe him so he and Jake take matters into their
own hands. This is the fifteenth story in Hazel Townson's
popular series about the boy detectives.

0 86264 624 3   80pp

The ARTHUR VENGER series by Hazel Townson,
 illustrated by David McKee

COUGHDROP CALAMITY

Inventor Arthur Venger and his two young helpers produce a cure
for the common cold, but they have reckoned without the
unscrupulous Bruno Kopman who will go to any lengths to
preserve his Comical Cough Sweet business.

0 86264 834 3   96pp

THE ONE-DAY MILLIONAIRES

Arthur Venger has a brilliant new scheme to make everyone feel
more generous. But when villains cash in on his idea to make a
fortune for themselves, chaos ensues. 'A funny and fast-paced
story for fluent readers.' - *Independent on Sunday*

0 86264 835 1   96pp

THE SPECKLED PANIC

When Kip Slater buys *truth*paste instead of *tooth*paste, he and his
friend Herbie soon realise the sensational possibilities of the
purchase. They plan to feed the truthpaste disguised in a cake to
the guest of honour at their school Speech Day but, unfortunately,
the headmaster eats the cake first ...
'Funny and vigorous.' - *Time Out*
This popular story has never been out of print since it was first
published in 1982.

0 86264 828 9   80pp